T0196491

ALSO BY DAVID PERLSTEIN

Fiction

Flight of the Spumonis
The Boy Walker
San Café
Slick!

* * *

Non-fiction

God's Others: Non-Israelites' Encounters
With God in the Hebrew Bible

Solo Success: 100 Tips for Becoming a
$100,000-a-Year Freelancer

The ODD PLIGhT OF ADONIS LIChT

A NOVEL

DAVID PERLSTEIN

THE ODD PLIGHT OF ADONIS LICHT

iUniverse books may be ordered through booksellers or by contacting:

iUniverse
1663 Liberty Drive
Bloomington, IN 47403
www.iuniverse.com
1-800-Authors (1-800-288-4677)

ISBN: 978-1-5320-1716-2 (sc)
ISBN: 978-1-5320-1743-8 (e)

Print information available on the last page.

iUniverse rev. date: 02/20/2017

For the guys.

"For the great majority of mankind are satisfied
with appearances, as though they were realities,
and are more often influenced by the things
that 'seem' than by those that 'are'."
Niccolo Machiavelli

Reality is merely an illusion, albeit a very persistent one.
Albert Einstein

1

h ad Adonis Licht known that the moonlit tumult outside his apartment window presaged a warping of the universe that would animate his fantasies beyond the extent of his imagination, he would have buried his head under his pillow. Instead, he rose in his bed, stilled his breathing and listened. The uproar evoked the digital carnage of a video game—the *whap-whap-whap* of rotors on helicopter gunships accompanied by commandos shrieking for blood. Adonis rummaged among his synapses for a peace-inducing remedy, one of the chants offered to the gods long ago by his mother. Finding the storerooms of his memory vacant, he gulped air until his lungs threatened to shatter his breastbone. Upon release he believed, a cry, a shout, a roar would put the unseen invaders to flight. A still, small voice nudged aside his resolve, cautioning *What about the hour?* Much as he might have wished to, he could not dismiss it. Adonis Licht was a reasonable man, a sensible, judicious man, a man who, with some years to go before being tethered to the numbing habits of middle age, dutifully accepted the responsibilities of adulthood. For five years, he had been a good neighbor. A quiet man. A man seldom noticed. Softly, he exhaled.

The ruckus grew louder.

Adonis sat up and reached towards his nightstand for his glasses. He dismissed any thought of turning on his lamp, fearing that this would lead sleep to elude him for the night's duration. Unless he *was* asleep.

He threw off his blanket and sprang to his feet. His hand found the cord to the window blinds and pulled. Glancing across the street, he found the apartment buildings opposite all shrouded in darkness. He drew his gaze closer and looked down.

A dozen or so pigeons, unmindful of the late-winter chill, occupied the ledge outside his window. Their decibel count increased.

Adonis rapped his knuckles on the dirt-streaked glass. The effort produced a brittle sound.

The pigeons swiveled their heads and glared defiantly.

He rapped again.

The glares hardened into those exhibited by unrepentant criminals in police mugshots.

Adonis rocked back on his heels. How could pigeons harden an expression? For that matter, how could pigeons display an expression? Still, he believed they had. The stuff of bad dreams? He pinched the flesh on the underside of his left arm just above the elbow.

Or thought he did.

"Goddamit!" he heard himself cry.

Or thought he did.

Tiny heads bobbed. The pigeons seemed to be chuckling.

In what world, Adonis wondered, did pigeons chuckle?

Seven measured paces—given the darkness, he counted as if he was blind—took him across the studio's floor to his lone closet. He reached inside and felt for the baseball bat he'd won as a child at a minor-league game. It proved to be the only baseball game he ever attended. Gripping the wooden handle, he pivoted back towards the window.

The commotion increased. Adamant about defending the territory they'd staked out on the ledge, the pigeons seemed not so much to coo as to bray. The sound evoked choirboys on the cusp of puberty.

Adonis squeezed the bat. No question, the pigeons had gotten into his head. How? The answer seemed obvious. Or at least, credible. Exhaustion. He was sure—or almost sure—that he'd stayed up past midnight. But since when did a man about to enter his mid-thirties find midnight too late an hour? Admittedly, he needed more sleep than he used to. He hadn't gotten it. Unless he was getting it now.

He considered pinching himself again but instead took seven steps back towards the window.

The great mystery remained. From where had the pigeons come? He'd rented the studio after coming to the city and landing his job at the Museum. Like all urbanites, including new ones like himself, he understood that pigeons flew roughshod over the city—feathered street gangs, brash and swaggering. Yet until now, they'd never appeared on—let alone overrun—the ledge outside his window. Not, at least, that he knew about.

A sense of fury—unfamiliar for the most part—tore through Adonis. He was, by his own admission, a mild-mannered man. Yet here he stood—or dreamed he stood—ready to swing or poke or otherwise wield a lethal weapon to force the withdrawal of unwanted intruders a fraction of his size but massed in numbers. He raised the bat.

The pigeons held their ground.

It occurred to Adonis that the pigeons understood the folly of his threat. For one thing, the window remained closed. Still, the bat was in his hand, the ball in his court.

He placed the bat on his bed. Then, grasping the window's handles, he pulled up. The sash elevated several inches then balked. He banged the frame with the heels of his palms.

3

The pigeons gaped. If pigeons could gape.

Adonis squatted to gain leverage and clutched the sash with both hands. He took a deep breath, released it with considered deliberation and stood. Or attempted to stand. A multitude of unwelcome sensations shot through his elbows, up his arms, across his shoulders and down his back. Pain flared in his knees. Determined, he applied every last ounce of muscle—what muscle he could claim given his status as a wide-body built for the more sedentary pursuits of art, music and literature.

The window might well have been a barbell set to an Olympic-record weight.

Adonis grunted. Or thought he grunted. Sweat beaded on his forehead.

The window, like the pigeons, maintained its defiance.

Adonis released his grip.

The pigeons strutted like gray-shirted fascists. Having communicated their disdain, they adopted a carefree mood and milled about, cooing softly as if making small talk at a cocktail party.

"Goddam you, motherfuckers!" Adonis heard himself scream. Or thought he did. His cheeks flushed. At least, he thought they did.

He feared having wakened his neighbors, whose responses might range from unpleasant to hostile. A small rationalization extended a measure of comfort. In major cities, the concept of *neighbor* could be defined as sketchy. Furthermore, who was going to confront a man who screamed curses when everyone else was asleep?

Defeated, he collapsed on his bed.

A pigeon jerked its head into the narrow opening above the sill.

Adonis reached for the bat.

The pigeon's head bobbed up and down. It appeared to be laughing.

He waved the bat half-heartedly.

Refusing to capitulate but apparently willing to concede that Adonis had been tormented up to and perhaps beyond his limit, the pigeon withdrew.

The back of Adonis' head burrowed into his pillow. He closed his eyes, although he could not determine the probability that he had just experienced an illusion. Whether awake or dreaming, he found affixed to the undersides of his eyelids images of pigeons laughing, strutting, mocking. What, he wondered, had he done to have rats with wings— real or imagined—devastate his night's sleep?

A period of calm passed, unmeasured and indeterminate. The blue-gray of first light streamed through the lower part of the window. Anticipating the musical throb of his cell phone alarm, Adonis opened his eyes and, not unlike his antagonists real or imaginary, cocked his head. The dissonance of workday traffic greeted him. His head dropped back on the pillow. While he seemed to have sweated through his tee shirt and shorts, he reassured himself that the episode *had* been a dream.

Although why was he cradling his baseball bat?

Not long after sunrise, Adonis subjected his unruly hair to a final and meaningless swipe of a comb, secured the three locks to his apartment door and turned towards the stairs to deal with another day as a faceless cog in a celebrated wheel. The elevator out of service for the better part of a week, he clutched the railing as he walked with a measured pace down the three flights flanked by walls the color of his Grandma Sophie's split pea soup. He didn't mind taking the stairs, cracked and chipped as they were. Descent involved minimal effort and offered at least one advantage over those who lived on the floors above him. On returning home, ascending the stairs would require substantially more from him. On the plus side of the ledger—his mother was a student of ledgers—climbing the stairs would provide a measure of exercise to counter the weight he continued to add in small but steady increments.

An increase in girth was to be expected. Adonis spent most of his time seated in front of a laptop in the bowels of the Museum writing catalog copy, exhibition labels, brochures and teacher's guides. Emails with fellow department members, conservators and educators—their work demanded digital paper trails—also filled his workdays. Then there was the considerable time spent around the conference table. The Curator in Charge of the Department of Renaissance Art called her team together often. *To encounter each other in the flesh is supremely human, people. We are humanists, people.*

Regarding his weight, Adonis had fought the good fight then surrendered to the inevitable. After moving to the city, he took out a gym membership, hoping to work himself into reasonable shape and, no less important, meet women. Not beautiful women. They would always be beyond his reach. No, he sought a woman on his own modest level. With luck, a level higher.

Within weeks he concluded that above the gym's entry might have been inscribed: *All hope abandon, ye who enter here.* He would never make the virile, confident impression exhibited by all those athletic men running the treadmill or striding the elliptical and enlarging their upper bodies with various machines recalling medieval torture devices. He sought and found a plausible excuse to miss a workout. One excuse led to another, which at least exercised his creativity. He abandoned hope for good.

From time to time, guilt plagued him. A metaphoric finger pointed to him as the Licht that failed. Again. When he was a child, his parents continually reminded him that they enjoyed good health and boundless energy thanks to uncompromising discipline. *To succeed in life, you have to be hard-nosed*, his mother insisted. Yoga and vegetarianism served as the pillars supporting their successful business. His mother pointed to his older brother as a proper example. Handsome and an accomplished athlete, Apollo still worked out daily and played ice hockey year-round. Given the random nature of genetic inheritance, Adonis avoided making comparisons.

He stepped down to the lobby floor with its checkerboard pattern of worn black and white tiles installed perhaps as early as the Eisenhower years. He found the entry door propped open.

Outside, the Building Manager retrieved a newspaper from the sidewalk. After straightening, she rolled her shoulders in protest of the small discomforts of age. She wore a green hand-knitted cardigan unraveling at the left elbow, a cream-colored blouse and a brown tweed skirt. She might have purchased her wardrobe from several nearby thrift shops.

To Adonis, the Building Manager represented something of a relic. Given her liberal application of bronze eye shadow, powder, blush and lipstick, she appeared to be anywhere between fifty and seventy. More likely, he thought, the latter—a milestone approached by his mother. Her hair brought to mind the redheaded angels in Titian's *Worship of Venus*.

The Building Manager rubbed the back of her neck.

Adonis joined her on the sidewalk.

7

She opened the newspaper's main section. Her eyes, a pale green reinforced by her sweater, flicked up at him then back down to the paper.

"Excuse me," he said.

"Elevator repair guy's coming next week," she said.

"It's not that. It's the pigeons."

"Pigeons?"

"Outside my window."

She turned the page. The newspaper crinkled. The sound suggested a predator crushing the bones of a small bird. Possibly a pigeon. If pigeons had predators. "Don't let this shock you," she said, "but the city's filled with pigeons."

"Yes, but I've never heard them outside my window before. They woke me in the middle of the night. I couldn't get back to sleep." He sniffled.

The Building Manager lowered the newspaper. "Tissue?" Without waiting for an answer, she extracted one from beneath her sweater's left sleeve.

Adonis slipped the tissue into his jacket pocket. "I don't like pigeons," he said.

She scowled.

"Not on the ledge outside my window. All night. And the mess."

"And I'm supposed to do what?"

Adonis shifted his weight. He hoped to have time to walk to the Museum as he did most mornings unless rain or exceptional cold forced him onto the bus. Were it not for those walks, he'd likely balloon into Falstaff-like proportions. "You could call one of those pest-control companies," he said.

The Building Manager placed a finger on her lower lip. The motion implied that she took her tenants' concerns to heart as long as they didn't cause her to expend undue energy. "You're not happy here?"

Adonis was quite happy. His studio proved adequate for a single man who only occasionally hosted guests and never more than one at a time. Closet space was limited, but he owned little in the way of clothing or anything else other than books. Most of his contemporaries had forsaken paper for the digital world, but he remained something of an antediluvian. Volumes of art and art history filled several shelving units. Others squatted in stacks along the walls. For reasons of economy as well as space, the remainder of his reading took the form of e-books. He devoured mysteries by British and Scandinavian authors. A few African writers caught his imagination. Occasionally, he indulged in extended bouts of science fantasy. Rent was affordable since the neighborhood, while boasting interesting cafés and restaurants, had yet to fall prey to gentrification.

"So?" asked the Building Manager.

Adonis wondered if he detected a hint of menace. If a woman probably as old as his mother could be menacing. Although he often found his mother intimidating. He smiled to demonstrate his good intentions.

The Building Manager raised the newspaper. "Slip a note under my door, Light."

He sniffled again. "*Licht*. As if it was spelled L-i-c-k-e-d."

She peered over the top of the newspaper. "Whatever."

"Anyway, thanks," he said to stay on her good side.

She turned the page.

He started down the sidewalk. Something wet splattered his left shoulder.

2

exiting the café he stopped at every morning, Adonis glanced uncomfortably at his shoulder. He'd initially used the tissue given him by the Building Manager to soak up some of the pigeon shit that had found him as if he'd been laser-targeted. Following up with dampened napkins from the café almost disguised the attack.

Although the Museum was only a block ahead and his sleepless night left him drained, he turned the corner and approached a narrow, dead-end alley nearly devoid of sunlight. Its grime-crusted brick walls, despite their flat planes, created the illusion of towering trees in a forbidding, Brothers Grimm forest inhabited by giants, ogres and witches. The alley could well have been the point of intersection with another dimension.

Adonis held up a small cardboard tray holding two large lattes and two paper bags, each containing an apple turnover. One of each was for him. The others constituted gifts for Anna, who sat just inside the alley's entrance. He'd given her that name as a bit of wordplay relating to her anonymity despite a considerable degree of visibility. As to her real name, he thought asking to be inappropriate. She'd never offered it. She'd never spoken.

Most mornings he found Anna there perched like an apparition on a small folding stool, its legs hidden beneath her. She kept a dented grocery cart close. Black plastic bags stuffed to bursting spilled over the cart's sides. Adonis wondered if they contained remnants from another life. He supposed she spent nights in the alley. When she'd taken to the streets and why remained concealed.

He first noticed Anna several months after assuming his position at the Museum. He responded to her with a measure of disgust. She might well have emerged from the farther reaches of Tolkien's Middle-earth, enveloped as she appeared to be in multiple layers of clothing encased in industrial-size garbage bags with holes cut for her head and arms. A black wool cap hid the length and color of her hair. It descended far enough to cover her forehead and eyebrows. A black scarf concealed her neck and the lower half of her face. Black gloves obscured her hands. Black shoes and socks covered her feet.

Adonis could make out only her eyes—the irises as black as the shopping bags and accessories—the flesh beneath them and the bridge of her nose. The small revelation of a deep golden skin tone suggested vermillion and yellow ochre with touches of ultramarine and titanium white. A passerby might take away the impression of an ageless woman from a distant, exotic land. Or a character from a painting by Hieronymus Bosch.

A week later, he acknowledged that Anna was, after all, a human being. Contrite, he brought her a cup of coffee, which she accepted but did not drink in his presence. The next week, he brought coffee and a pastry. This became a weekly ritual. He assumed that she devoured his gifts after he left to avoid revealing herself, a situation he found disappointing at first but one to which he soon acquiesced. By the end of his first year at the Museum, the frequency of his offerings rose to two mornings a week. Sometimes three. She'd reveal the hint of a nod and a glint in those black eyes. Beyond that,

Anna maintained the contemplative silence of a cloistered nun. But if she would not—or could not—speak, she provided Adonis a cherished gift. Unlike his mother, she listened.

"Big meeting today," said Adonis.

Anna's gaze encouraged him to continue.

His right eye began to tear. He sniffled. He realized he'd forgotten to bring napkins from the café. "I really don't feel comfortable in meetings."

The Curator in Charge of the Department of Renaissance Art set coffee in china cups at the far end of the polished teak conference table—one before the Museum Director and the other before the Chief Curator.

Adonis' eyes followed her return to her seat. He knew it unwise to stare. Still, he couldn't help himself. The Curator in Charge, who happened to be his boss, drew attention to herself, wanted or not. That, Adonis believed, made the two of them polar opposites.

A feeling of self-consciousness crept over Adonis unrelated to the Curator in Charge's striking appearance, which always left him a little uneasy. She'd advised him and his fellow Curatorial Assistant to dress casually for the meeting. In response, he'd chosen a blue oxford shirt to go with his usual khakis. Now he felt like a child at the adults' table.

The Museum Director, as always, struck Adonis as being as imposing as a four-star general. He wore a dark gray suit, white shirt with blue pinstripes and navy tie displaying the museum's logo in gold. The Chief Curator, to whom all departmental Curators in Charge reported, wore a blue blazer, white shirt and crimson tie along with gray slacks—a wardrobe choice both impeccable and subtly deferential.

For her part, the Curator in Charge dressed in a simple white blouse revealing a hint of cleavage. More than a hint, Adonis thought. It and a navy skirt displayed her figure to full advantage. Her Administrative Assistant, who had stepped out of the room, wore a more modest blouse and flowing skirt.

The Curator in Charge turned to Adonis. "Be a dear and pour me a coffee, would you? The African blend. And you're not coming down with something, are you?"

Adonis shook his head. If a cold was trying to infiltrate his system, he'd fight it off. In five years at the Museum, he'd taken only two or three sick days. Following her request—or was it a command?—he circled the table to a cart containing two containers of coffee, a large bowl of mixed fruit and a tray of small, elegant pastries. The Museum Director having passed, the fruit and pastries remained untouched.

"Soy milk," called the Curator in Charge.

Adonis complied.

The Administrative Assistant reentered the room and sat.

The Curator in Charge nodded as Adonis placed the coffee in front of her. "Thank you, Adonis," she said.

The Museum Director turned to the Chief Curator. "Shouldn't we have placed someone named Adonis in the Department of Antiquities?"

The Chief Curator smiled. As did the Curator in Charge, the Assistant Curator in Charge, the Administrative Assistant and the Communications Director, who wore a matching gray skirt and jacket. The male Curatorial Assistant with whom Adonis worked on the project to be discussed smirked.

"My parents named me Adonis because they have degrees in the Classics. They were double majors, actually. Classics and Asian Studies." He remembered offering that same explanation at two previous meetings. Possibly three. He assumed he'd have to offer it again—and that ten minutes after the meeting, both the Museum Director and the Chief Curator would be unable to pick him out of a random group of employees.

The Museum Director's lips barely curved upward as if he was greeting the hundredth guest on a reception line. "Yes, of course." He turned to the Chief Curator then to the Curator in Charge. "So where do we stand?"

The Curator in Charge nodded to the Administrative Assistant who turned down the lights. A PowerPoint slide filled a large screen. It bore the title *Madonna and Child: The Love of Beauty, the Beauty of Love*. The Museum's upcoming exhibition would showcase paintings of Mary and the infant Jesus—all acknowledged as masterpieces—from around the world. The exhibition would run from mid-autumn through mid-winter before transferring to a collaborating institution sharing its expertise and the considerable costs involved.

Adonis, having done considerable legwork on the exhibition along with his fellow Curatorial Assistant, focused his attention on the Curator in Charge. She could have been taken for a brunette version of Botticelli's Venus. True, she was older than Venus. Older than him for that matter but not more than forty. Early forties tops. Like a goddess, she defied age. Her figure aroused his fantasies, although it often left him with the impression less of erotic curves than sharp angles. Most intriguing, her left foot turned slightly in. From time to time she walked with a barely detectable limp. Adonis found this oddly alluring. Perfection, he considered, might be a greater flaw.

A slide came up of a masterpiece held by a private collector.

The Curator in Charge pressed her palms together. Even in the near-dark, her face glowed. "Wonderful news," she said. "I'm pleased, thrilled, honored, overjoyed to announce that Clark Merrill, one of the city's most prominent business leaders and a member of our board, has agreed to donate the painting we've been talking about for so long. It's the breathtaking Madonna and Child by the sixteenth-century German Norbertus of Hannover, who's had the art world buzzing these last few years."

Murmurs of approval rang out around the table.

"I don't have to tell you that the competition was fierce. Despite Mr. Merrill's relationship with the Museum, another institution with rather grand ambitions nearly secured the painting. Let's just say that I snatched away Mr. Merrill's commitment in the nick of time."

The lights went up.

The Museum Director clasped his hands. "I'm very pleased. We're *all* very pleased. That painting going anywhere else would have been an embarrassment."

Heads nodded in unison.

The Communications Director cleared her throat. "And what valuation will we announce?"

The Curator in Charge beamed. "The appraiser puts it at thirty-five million."

"A nice little tax deduction," said the Museum Director.

"Of course, that's less than half the price of Holbein the Younger's *Darmstadt Madonna* at auction in 2011. Not even close to the Modigliani that brought a hundred-and-seventy million with fees at Christie's in 2015."

"Impressive enough," said the Museum Director. "And provenance?" He looked down the table at Adonis. "I take it provenance has been wrapped up?"

At lunchtime, Adonis found a table in a far corner of the Museum's basement café. If he ever rose to Assistant Curator, he'd be privileged to eat in the members dining room. But that leap might take years. And even if he could ward off the competition, the promotion probably would be his last at the Museum.

A Ph.D. remained a possibility if programs didn't dismiss his undergrad and graduate work at run-of-the-mill public universities. His parents could have covered the tuition at any prestigious private school, but his mother had baulked. *You go off to one of those hotshot schools and you lose the common touch. Your father and I kept that. We made it work for us.* That said, his parents met at an expensive private university heralded for its academic standing and liberal bent. His mother frequently boasted that her parents wrote all the checks. *Your father's parents? Timid people. They always struggled. Your father went on scholarship.* Whether she was proud or dismissive of that, Adonis remained unsure.

So, a doctorate. And then what? He acknowledged lacking the drive and political cunning of his Curator in Charge. Or, for that matter, his mother and brother, whose undergraduate degrees proved sufficient to their purposes. They were strivers, trampling obstacles like bull elephants in heat. Yet some surprise might lie ahead. After all, his father, as laid-back as they came, built the family fortune.

Adonis returned to his sandwich: grilled vegetables and feta cheese on focaccia. A healthy choice. Chips balanced things out. His mother disapproved of chips unless the potatoes were organic and baked. Making the case for quality of life, he ripped the bag open.

The other Curatorial Assistant who'd attended the morning's meeting dropped into the seat opposite.

Only now did it occur to Adonis that the Curatorial Assistant wore a shirt with alternating inch-wide mauve and pink stripes. Second thoughts leaped out at him. He'd chosen his blue oxford to demonstrate his seriousness. Blue symbolized royalty and authority since blue dyes—like pigments—once were difficult to obtain and thus expensive. Artists found blue in abundance with the commercial manufacture of Prussian blue in 1823. Had he left the higher-ups with the impression that he was stodgy and unimaginative? A more strategic choice would have been his mock Mondrian with its squares and rectangles of red, yellow and, yes, blue. Primary colors. Powerful colors. Or would the mock Mondrian have colored him quirky, the antithesis of a team player? Why not an orange jumpsuit?

The Curatorial Assistant narrowed his eyes. "What's in the bag?"

"Another sandwich."

"For?"

"Someone."

"That someone being a semi-exotic Asian type who works the membership desk?"

Adonis feigned annoyance.

"No offense, but she's no beauty queen. That's why *semi-exotic*. But a warm body's a warm body."

Adonis made no effort to explain that he'd bought the sandwich for Anna.

"Anyway," said the Curatorial Assistant, "it's *your* ass."

Adonis stared.

"The provenance you did on Norbertus' Madonna and Child."

"*We* did. To make sure asses were covered."

"A *certain* ass. And a fine ass our Curator in Charge displays."

Adonis cast a look at the Curatorial Assistant like a father finding his son staring at naked women in a magazine and, remembering his own youth, unsure how to respond.

"Look, I'm not the only guy here who thinks this way," said the Curatorial Assistant. "The straight guys, anyway.

It's just that the Museum expects you to project this image of gentility, which is total bullshit. You ever really listen to our exalted Museum Director? Besides, you know the kind of lives most artists lived. And whose work hangs on our walls? Anyway, someone with an incredible ass wanted to show the powers-that-be how she works her staff—you and me primarily—to the bone, leaves no stone unturned, climbs every mountain. Even fords every stream."

"You don't think those clichés are a bit worn?"

The Curatorial Assistant shrugged.

Adonis nodded. It had taken a major effort to unearth documentation relevant to ownership of the Norbertus painting. They'd even uncovered a letter from a marquis, who bought the painting before the French Revolution and an unanticipated encounter with the guillotine. It detailed a previously unknown work by an obscure German artist elevated into the pantheon only in the mid-twentieth century. The Virgin cradled the infant Jesus in a garden of Italianate design. Green hills rose in the background. Clouds dotted a blue sky in which—the work's signature feature—floated a palace. A noted German laboratory authenticated the letter.

The Curatorial Assistant smiled. "I'm just saying, shit happens. And you being low man on the totem pole, guess who takes the fall?"

3

N ear empty, the Museum lobby reflected the hiatus between afternoon and evening visitors. Across the marble floor, Adonis spotted the woman he'd come to see seated at the long marble counter. She wore the basic guest service outfit—navy sweater over white blouse.

He took a moment to compose himself—something never required of Apollo. He couldn't remember not envying his brother, even when in high school Apollo got Kimberly Hastings pregnant. Maybe *because* he got her pregnant. Their mother reduced the matter to a business transaction. *We'll pay for the abortion and give a little something to her parents, although they should be damn glad not to see their daughter disgraced.* For the first time, Adonis realized that Apollo not only dated cheerleaders, he screwed them. Although Kimberly Hastings was a volleyball player. To no one's surprise, Apollo married a woman who turned heads. They propagated a son and a daughter, each of whom drew gushing praise from passing strangers. Even as an adult, Apollo teased that Adonis wasn't really a Licht. *Someone left a baby on the doorstep.* On occasions when people saw the two of them together, they seemed dumbstruck to learn they were brothers.

Adonis ran the fingers of his right hand through his hair then crossed the floor. He reminded himself to smile.

The woman looked up.

"Hi, Emily," he said in a near-whisper.

"Well, this is a surprise," she said. "Working late tonight?"

"Heading home."

"Wish *I* was. I'm just getting my head together for the next wave. People can be so..."

Adonis nodded. He met the public only infrequently and found that arrangement to his liking. On those occasions when he spoke to members or school groups, he summoned the only advice he could remember offered by his father. *A smile and a shoeshine. Willy Loman. Death of a Salesman.* Having read the play and seen a college production, Adonis found the advice unnerving. Willy Loman was a frightened man, a fraud who crafted an image to fool his family. A man who *knew* he was a fraud. Willy Loman believed—or thought he believed—that a smile and a shoeshine could divert people's attention, show them what they wanted to see and win them over. *Except maybe for the shoeshine*, his father said, pointing down to his hemp sandals.

"So home, huh?" said Emily.

Adonis feared this wasn't going well. "I'm kind of beat. I'll heat up some ramen. Drink some green tea. Listen to music. Read. Close my eyes early."

Emily nodded. "Get your rest. Stuff's still going around." Her eyes shifted to the bag containing Anna's sandwich.

"For a friend," he said. "An older woman."

She raised an eyebrow.

"*Old* woman. She doesn't get around much."

"That's sweet. Anyway, what kind of day was it downstairs?"

"Like most. Lots going on."

"Like?"

Adonis found Emily's question encouraging but problematic. A directive had been given that the Norbertus acquisition wasn't to be discussed in-house let alone made public. "I'm sworn to secrecy."

She covered her mouth with an exaggerated motion of her hand. "The big acquisition," she whispered.

Adonis swallowed.

"Word gets around."

"But there hasn't been an official announcement."

"So you really can't tell me anything?"

"Some things you can't tell just anyone."

Emily's eyes registered a chill as if what passed for a small flame had been doused with water.

Adonis looked away. And what color were her eyes anyway? Hazel? Gray like his own? Certainly not a sparkling blue. Brown probably. Asians had brown eyes. Probably brown. Truth be told, he didn't think her eyes were all that attention getting. Not that he found anything wrong with her appearance. She hardly compared to any of Bronzino's nudes or the Mary of Bellini's *Barbarigo Altarpiece*. Still, was he flattering himself to think she might be attracted to him? Not that he was Quasimodo from Hugo's *The Hunchback of Notre Dame*. More like the overlooked narrator in Ralph Ellison's *Invisible Man*. Or someone people physically couldn't see like Griffin in Wells' *The Invisible Man*, although that was science fiction. He liked to think that his mother would rate him relatively high on the appearance scale, but she held as firm a grip on praise as Scrooge on pounds, shillings and pence.

So maybe Emily represented a bit of a reach. On this day, however, Adonis' confidence felt less fragile. "There's this Cuban-Chinese restaurant," he said. Generally, he didn't eat at places that adventurous, but being taken as ordinary could easily lead to rejection.

"You think because I'm Chinese I eat Chinese food all the time?"

His cheeks flushed.

"Kidding," she said.

"Saturday night?"

She stared at him like a television game show contestant puzzled by a question she'd only half expected.

Still, he noted, she didn't say no.

On returning from work, Adonis rang the Building Manager's bell.

She opened her door just enough to reveal a scowl.

Adonis set his jaw to achieve an expression firm but not threatening. Not that he believed he could ever project any meaningful degree of danger. "I thought I'd check in about the pest-control people," he said.

She glowered as if Adonis had mounted the barricades and hoisted a placard airing a list of grievances with the intent of overthrowing the long-established regime. "All this crap about tenants' rights," she returned. "Landlords have rights, too. My employers, they have rights. I know my job. I can do my job, thank you."

Adonis' jaw dropped. "It's just... I thought maybe you might have scheduled something while I was at work."

"What? You think I don't have other tenants making a fuss about this and that and God knows what? And people coming by looking for an apartment in an affordable building offering this kind of location?" She pointed a finger at his chest. "You think you're special?"

"It's just a phone call."

"As simple as that, huh? You think everyone should just drop everything because you have a little problem. Or what you *think* is a problem. Entitled. That's the word for you young people. Well, maybe you haven't thought about it, but I'm still trying to light a fire under the elevator people."

Adonis shocked himself by finding his fist clenched. He pressed it against his thigh. Still, he wondered what it would feel like to press his knuckles against her chin and warn her that this would be the last job she'd ever hold unless she responded to his simple request and right now. He dismissed the impulse. He wasn't that kind of person, although he often wished he was. His parents praised themselves as *mellow*, but he'd seen how determined and unrelenting they could be when they wanted something. Not so much his father, perhaps, but his mother. He wished he'd inherited her resolve. Her doggedness. But what would he accomplish with an act of untoward aggression? He'd been lucky to find the studio. With rents rising in the area, he'd never be able to afford another apartment unless he shared it with someone. Perhaps someone like Emily. Only how likely was that? Not that he didn't enjoy entertaining the possibility.

The Building Manager pulled her glasses down to the end of her nose and peered at him over the frames. "So here's the way it is, Mr. Light..."

"Licht. Like, the boy *licked* the ice cream." Hadn't he recently told her that? "Although it means light."

"Light as in something that shines or as in weightless, insubstantial, not much there?"

Adonis sought to deflect what he considered a touch of disdain. Maybe something of a microaggression, a big catchword on campuses these days. "As in turn on the light," he said. "But it's pronounced *Licked*. You know me. I'm in three-oh-two."

"Oh, yes. I know you, Licht as in *Licked* three-oh-two. Only here's how it is. I'll get to it. Might take a week. Might take two. Might take more."

"So should I check back with you next week?"

She frowned then held out a tissue.

23

Adonis left his hands at his sides.

"It's not used," she said.

He took the tissue and swiped it across his nose.

"I'll make a note of our little discussion, Licht three-oh-two. And while I'm at it, I'll check when your lease is up."

4

Twilight lingered outside the bathroom window as Adonis stepped out of the shower and wrapped himself in a towel grown too small to easily remain affixed to his body. His heart threatened to leap from his chest. He was that excited. *Stoked* came into his head. He imagined Apollo felt the same way when he charged out of the locker room before a football game in high school.

It was Saturday night. Adonis had a date.

His dates being only occasional, he intended to make the most of it. If the stars were with him. Not that he took literally astrology or soothsaying or anything supernatural. His parents had. His father always. Over the years, his mother discarded the mystical like the commander of a crowded lifeboat pushing away the hands of desperate survivors bobbing in the water and clutching at the sides— then throwing overboard the people inside the boat. No, whatever happened would be up to him. Adonis Licht was a free agent. His own man.

He examined his face in the mirror and pondered whether he should shave. Perplexed, he leaned forward. Something—not his whiskers, which had barely sprouted since the morning—seemed off. He squinted. The muscles at the tops of his cheeks began to ache. He closed his eyes and let his jaw go slack. Seeking to slow his pulse, he took five deep breaths. Then another five. Satisfied, he opened his eyes.

The mirror revealed nothing. Yet something in his reflection failed to register. He wondered if the sleep deprivation he suffered at the hands—or wings—of the pigeons squatting on the ledge had triggered a minor hallucination. Still, he'd slept for two hours after the pigeons flew off that morning and taken an afternoon nap.

Adonis retrieved his glasses from his nightstand and returned to the mirror. He was no hypochondriac, but he couldn't help wondering if his forehead, cheeks and jaw each displayed a small measure of disfigurement generated by the early stages of some dreaded disease. He examined his skin for a minor eruption that might indicate an unwelcome resurgence of adolescence.

He saw nothing.

The observation offering scant comfort, Adonis gave the lenses of his glasses a swipe with his towel then returned once more to his reflection. His eyes seemed the same gray. *They're kind of leaden, no offense,* a former almost-girlfriend once confided. *You know. Like the sky just before it starts to rain really hard.* His complexion remained clear if borderline sallow. His cheeks maintained their same fullness. His nose displayed its perceptible arc—a testament to family genetics. As always, his chin appeared devoid of prominence.

He dropped the towel. The paunch he'd developed—even nurtured—as an undergraduate protruded as if in the early stages of pregnancy. The sagging flesh gave the impression of a suit several sizes too large and in need of pressing. He raised and lowered his shoulders. They appeared no less stooped. *Posture,* his mother reminded him on his annual visits home, *is absolutely essential to a person's health.*

Good posture also makes you look taller. Tall people make a better impression. They get ahead. Look at your brother.

Adonis put the razor away. Many television and movie stars along with athletes maintained three-day growths or closely trimmed beards. This created the aura of a free spirit, an adventurous risk-taker, a man to be admired and perhaps also feared. He grimaced. Previous efforts at growing a beard produced only random patches of hair evocative of a drought-stricken lawn. More important, his Curator in Charge frowned upon stubble. *We have an image to project, people.*

He sniffled. He sniffled again. He brushed his nose with the back of his hand. For days, he'd seemed to be on the verge of coming down with something. He nodded to himself. That had to be it.

Only he couldn't abandon the feeling that he *had* seen something different in the mirror. He didn't know what. But *something.*

As they walked, Adonis kept Emily to his left, nearer the curb. He'd read—or heard—that a man should walk on the building side of a sidewalk to offer protection from muggers who might leap from the shadows of a doorway or alley. Or the opposite was true. Threats came from the street. He was never sure about these things.

Screaming stopped their progress.

Across the boulevard, the amber glow of a streetlamp spotlighted a man in a tattered overcoat shuffling backward reminiscent of Michael Jackson's moonwalk. His face scanned the night sky as he bellowed, "White bitch! White faggot!"

Adonis fingered his cell. But what, he thought, was the point of calling the police? It stood to reason that someone else would. Or had. Besides, he'd failed to locate the targets of the man's invective. Apparently, they existed only in the man's imagination. Other pedestrians reinforced his conclusion, continuing to scurry here and there at their normal pace.

Still, Adonis took Emily by the arm.

"Life in the big city," she said.

At the corner, a chill breeze fondled Adonis' neck. He worried that he'd dressed too lightly, although a streak of mild weather suggested that spring would arrive sooner rather than later. The thought returned to him that he might be coming down with a fever. He certainly didn't want Emily to catch anything. At the same time, he couldn't pass up the opportunity she'd given him.

The light turned green. They crossed and ducked under a gold awning. Adonis opened the door to the restaurant.

"I'm not sure you're supposed to do that," Emily said. "It's like... an anti-feminist throwback thing."

As she went through the door, something brushed by Adonis' shoulders.

Several diners muttered mild epithets. A woman shrieked. As did a man. Others laughed.

A pigeon flew counter-clockwise around the restaurant.

The host, a Chinese man with graying hair, took a white towel off his forearm and waved it like a policeman directing traffic.

The pigeon flew out the door.

The diners resumed their meals. Conversations hummed.

The host sat them at a table with a dark wood top, varnished and slightly pitted. He wiped the table with the same white towel and set down paper napkins rolled around forks and plastic chopsticks. Then he presented menus.

Emily slipped out of her coat. The neckline of her pink dress exposed the upper part of her chest against which rested a delicate gold chain. A pink cardigan, left open, covered her shoulders.

Adonis joined her in taking a measure of the restaurant. The walls, mauve and green, displayed framed black-and-white photos of Old Havana—the baroque cathedral, the domed El Capitolio, the Plaza Vieja. Speakers suspended from the ceiling gave full voice to a pre-Castro jazz band. The piano rippled like waves in the harbor.

"Great place," said Emily. "Even the pigeons like it." She leaned forward. "You feel okay?"

Despite feeling slightly under the weather, Adonis rallied his spirits and nodded. An entire evening lay ahead. "I thought we could start with mojitos. Then dumplings and spicy fried calamari. Then steak with 'dark' fried rice. It's the house special."

She rested a hand on the chain around her neck. "You did your homework."

Among other things, he'd learned that the owners were Chinese who grew up in Havana. He hoped that Emily would not think him condescending. Then again, she'd accepted his invitation, and he'd been quite specific about the restaurant.

The waiter brought their mojitos and the dumplings.

Emily lifted her glass. "To art."

Adonis touched his glass to hers then sipped. He planned to pace himself. More than that, restrict himself to a single drink. He had little tolerance for alcohol. As to Emily, that was another story. She could down as many mojitos as she wanted. The more the better. He laughed softly.

Emily cocked her head. "Is something dribbling down my chin?"

"No. God, I'm sorry. It's... I just realized I don't know your last name."

"I wear a name tag at work."

"I guess I never looked. That sounds weird, doesn't it?"

"Actually, it only has my first name." She picked up a dumpling with her chopsticks.

Adonis used his fingers.

"It's easy," she said. "Chopsticks."

"For you maybe."

"It's not like I learned from my parents."

"Oh. I thought... You know."

"They only use chopsticks in Chinese restaurants. Our name... my name... is LaRoche."

The dumpling slipped from Adonis' fingers. "You're *not* Chinese?"

"As Chinese as the people who own this place. Genetically, anyway. I'm adopted."

Adonis picked up the dumpling.

"My dad... my adoptive dad... he's Swiss. Born in America. You know how that goes. My mom's Welsh-German. What about you?"

A simmering heat spread over Adonis' cheeks.

"Greek, I'd guess," she continued. "Adonis and all. Although Licht doesn't sound Greek."

"Not Greek. No. My grandparents, both sets, they were Jewish."

"Cool. In college, I took this course in Jewish fiction. I remember this novel about what they call *just men*. Just as in justice or righteous or something like that. There was this other name for them. A Hebrew name or something. I don't remember. Anyway, these *just men*, they're the people who keep the world going. Without them..." She held her hands in front of her, fingertips touching, then pulled them apart. "*Poof!* Only they're not heroes or rich people or anything like that. No one knows who they are. *They* don't even know who they are. They can be street people or crazy people or anybody. Do you do any Jewish stuff?"

Adonis shook his head. "About all my folks did was have my brother Apollo and me circumcised."

"Apollo?"

"He's older. He works for a company that develops business software. Vice president of marketing."

"Apollo and Adonis. Wow." Emily pushed the remains of a dumpling around her plate. "So anyway, circumcision. If you don't mind my asking, that's a very Jewish thing, right?"

"My folks didn't particularly care, but they didn't want to upset my grandparents."

"Was there a rabbi or something?"

"A doctor."

"So that was it?"

"Pretty much. Except when I was a kid, my dad would light these candles."

"Sabbath candles? I read about that."

"No, these other candles. They come in a glass. It's around the size of a shot glass."

Late one winter afternoon, Adonis watched his father strike a wooden match. *This candle in the glass, it's called a yahrzeit. It's for Grandpa.—But Grandpa's dead.—That's why. You light a yahrzeit on the anniversary of someone's death. Every year.—Why?—Because that's what Grandpa and Grandma did for their parents. All they could do, really.—Why?—You light a yahrzeit to help you remember someone you love after they die.—Don't you think about Grandpa anyway?—Sure. It's just...—Will I light a...—Yahrzeit.—Will I light a candle for you after you die?—I don't know. That's up to you.*

Emily looked pensive. "Were your parents... or maybe your grandparents..." She pressed her hand against her lips. "You know."

Adonis nodded. He knew that his father's parents survived the Holocaust but nothing more. His father told him only that his grandparents met in a displaced persons camp and, after coming to the United States, shortened their name to Licht. "From Lichtenberg, maybe. Or Lichtenstein. I don't know. It's water under the bridge."

As a small boy, however, Adonis saw something he'd come to understand only as an adult. One summer morning beneath a tree in his parents' backyard, his father's father sat with him on a wooden bench his father had made. Despite weather appropriate to a steam bath, his grandfather wore long sleeves. With a sudden motion, his grandfather slapped his own forearm. Then he unbuttoned his cuff and pushed up the sleeve. Adonis saw not only the Rorschach-like remains of an insect but also blue numbers. He neither knew what the numbers signified nor how to ask about them. His grandfather, exhibiting a look of pain beyond that generated by a mosquito bite, rolled the sleeve back down. Adonis joined him in an unspoken pact of silence.

"What about your mother's folks?"

His mother's parents—her father the owner of a department store—liquidated their assets and bribed their way out of Germany in 1938, a year before the invasion of Poland. They prospered in America. His mother never spoke about her grandparents.

"Did any of them do Jewish stuff?"

"Not really. As far as my parents go, *The Iliad* was their Bible. That and the *Vedas*. After college, they spent three years at an ashram in southern India."

"So that's why they named you Adonis. The Greek stuff and all. Is your middle name one of those Hindu gods like with all the arms or an elephant's trunk?"

"It's Elijah. My parents chose it in memory of my mother's father's father. They wanted to please my grandfather. He loaned them money."

"So anyway, what are your folks now? Are they Hindus or something?"

He shook his head, partly to answer her question and partly to clear his mind slightly fogged by the mojito. "They used to say they were just spiritual. My mother not so much anymore. My father passed two years ago."

Despite maintaining a strict diet and exercise regimen, Adonis' father suffered a massive coronary while meditating. *Obviously,* his mother insisted, more in tune with her past than she'd been in some time, *a genetic time bomb triggered by all the poisons people have spilled into the earth.*

Emily pressed her lips together.

"We scattered his ashes in the pond on their estate."

Emily placed a hand on Adonis' wrist. "Listen, you don't mind if I order another drink? Some people think that Chinese can't hold their liquor, but that's bullshit."

Adonis smiled. A second drink or a third—even a fourth—represented a small investment that could pay big dividends.

"Anyway, you said an estate?"

"After my folks came back from India they lived on this commune. Then they borrowed money from my grandfather to open a store in the town nearby."

"Were you around then?"

"We lived in an apartment upstairs until I was around three. It's a little hazy. Then they bought a house nearby. I remember that. When I was around six, we moved to the city where I grew up. It's a lot smaller than here."

The waiter set another mojito in front of Emily and looked at Adonis.

Adonis shook his head.

"But an estate?" Emily asked.

"They ended up with something like twenty-seven stores in four states. When I finished grad school, they sold to a conglomerate. That's when they bought the estate."

"With the pond where...?"

"And a pool, a tennis court and a yoga studio. And a five-car garage."

"They had five cars? Hippies?"

"A motor home, too. They sold it after a few months, though. My mother prefers hotels."

Emily paused to relish the steak and dark fried rice. "So your brother, Apollo. Did you guys get along?"

Adonis scratched the back of his neck. "He used to push me around a lot. Once, he hit me on the back with a piece of rubber hose. In movies, they say a hose doesn't leave marks. It does."

"What did your parents do?"

"I never told them." What, he reasoned, would be the point? Apollo would have hit him again. Harder. "Although my mother once saw Apollo push me off my bike."

Emily leaned in. "And?"

"She made us meditate a whole hour every morning before school. Both of us. For a week."

The waiter picked up the empty plates that had contained the dumplings and the calamari.

"Another mojito?" Adonis asked.

"God no. Well, I wouldn't mind, but I don't think so."

Adonis folded his hands in his lap.

"So aren't you going to say something?" she asked.

Adonis' heart raced. "About what?"

"The big acquisition."

Adonis chewed his lips then relaxed. "I can tell you some things, but you can't tell anyone else. Not until the Communications Department releases the story."

She smiled. "Why would I tell anyone?"

"It's *The Madonna of the Heavenly Palace* by Norbertus of Hannover. Late sixteenth century. The colors are very Roman, way brighter than those in northern German palettes. The northern Europeans' light was darker. Like their psyches. Norbertus had this very distinctive technique, too. The thing is, following the Reformation, there was very little demand for religious art in the German states. The piece is pretty rare, if you know what I mean. Only a dozen of Norbertus' works are known to have survived."

Emily propped her elbow on the table and rested her chin in her palm. "Were you involved?"

"Another curatorial assistant... maybe you know him... Fred? Fred and I worked on the provenance."

She wrinkled her nose.

"Where the painting came from. This wealthy donor acquired the painting at auction years ago. We gathered up documentation going back to the late nineteen-forties. That's when the paper trail stops."

"And Mr. Generous is?"

"Honestly, I can't tell you. For a few more days, anyway."

The waiter cleared the table.

"So I was thinking," Adonis said. "Maybe you'd like to come up to my apartment."

"You have your own place?"

Apollo nodded.

"How can you afford it?"

"It's a studio. In an old building. I got lucky."

"So you figure you'll get lucky tonight?"

Adonis swallowed hard.

"We had a good time," Emily said. "But on the first date?"

"I was thinking we could talk. I have a pretty big collection of art books."

She arched an eyebrow.

"I didn't say sex, did I?"

"Did you have to? My roommates, they'll hook up with anyone. It gets awkward since the four of us share two bedrooms. I'm more like, sex requires a commitment. Not a ring or anything like that. Just some kind of something happening between me and whoever. And I don't want to be a drama queen or anything, but I'm coming off a relationship. I broke up with a guy."

The waiter placed their check on the table.

Adonis reached for his wallet.

"We can split it," Emily said.

"I asked *you* out. And I've had a good time."

She wrinkled her nose again. "You take rejection pretty well."

5

The dream, lingering and intense, offered no replay— erotic or otherwise—of his date with Emily. Rather, a flock of pigeons—a winged horde—soared over rooftops, sailed between buildings and swooped down like missiles to torment scurrying humans. Adonis flew among them. He glided endlessly as time warped beyond recognition, impelled by a vague promise of something wonderful yet frightening beckoning just beyond the reach of his— Arms? Wings? Eyes lifted toward the sun, Adonis raced upward only, like Icarus, to be pulled back and plunge earthward with breath-sucking acceleration until, the moment of obliteration at hand, his head struck not the unforgiving pavement but his pillow.

Transitioning to a state of semi-wakefulness, Adonis rubbed away the thick crust gathered at the corners of his eyes and along the edges of his lids. He blinked then turned towards the window at his bedside. Morning light seeped through the blinds. He considered going back to sleep. Sunday was the one day he could sleep late without guilt. He clicked on his cell phone to check the time.

The numerals appeared blurred beyond recognition. He put on his glasses. The time still eluded him. He wiped the lenses with his tee shirt but achieved no better results. He returned the glasses to his nightstand then held the cell at arm's length. The numerals indicated 7:55 AM. The smaller day and date proved as impossible to decipher as legal text in a TV commercial. His glasses again proved useless. He entertained the thought that he'd come down with something given all the sniffling he'd done the past few days. Not that it mattered. He had all of Sunday to rest.

He thought of Emily and grinned. He'd enjoyed their date the night before. Naturally, he'd hoped that Emily would be asleep next to him this morning. Still, he remained optimistic. In baseball, they'd call her putting him off strike one. Fine. You got three strikes. He knew that much.

A sudden trembling overtook Adonis. He took a breath and attempted to focus his thoughts. He'd had colds before, but his vision had never suffered. What if he'd taken seriously ill? He slipped out from under the covers and stood. His knees threatened to buckle. He pressed a hand down on his nightstand to steady himself. Remaining motionless, he gathered his strength. When his legs grew sufficiently steady, he raised the blinds and held up his cell. The day and date remained indistinct. It occurred to him that that function might not be working. "What day is today?" he asked the voice command.

The answer came back without hesitation. "Today is Thursday..."

A sharp pain pierced the center of Adonis' forehead. He dropped onto the bed, took a deep breath and repeated his question. Displaying the obstinacy of an ideologue toeing the party line, the cell maintained that it *was* Thursday. His breathing accelerated. His fingertips tingled.

Was he to believe that he'd spent four days asleep? *More* than four days. More than four days totally disconnected from the world?

First the pigeons, then this.

He closed his eyes. Following what might have passed as a period of meditation, he opened his eyes and found his vision restored. He raised his right hand to his temple. He wasn't wearing his glasses. He stumbled towards the coffee table and lowered himself to the sofa. Seeking confirmation, he powered up his laptop. It too proclaimed the day Thursday.

Adonis shook his head. Four days asleep? Impossible. He considered that, as during the first night the pigeons launched their invasion, he had fallen victim to an illusion. But that didn't add up. The pigeons outside his window were quite real.

Turning back to his cell, he checked his recent calls. He discovered that he'd received none but made one—to the Assistant to the Curator in Charge just before ten Monday morning. The Monday morning that was supposed to be tomorrow. He had no memory of making the call let alone what he might have said.

Was he to believe that today *was* Thursday? That he'd become a contemporary Rip Van Winkle? If so, at least the department knew he was ill—if he'd called as the cell reported. That posed a question. What might he have told them? That he'd be out for the week? Or had he related some story of a death in the family or an unanticipated adventure as far-fetched as his four-day slumber? Had the Assistant to the Curator in Charge been sympathetic? And how had the Curator in Charge responded? Did the department miss him at the Museum? Did he still have a job?

Given that no one from the Museum had called back, he assumed he *did* have a job. Or at least the possibility of saving his job. But he'd have to move fast.

He stood. Unlike only a moment before, he felt light on his feet. Surefooted. He went back to the window by his bed. The ledge was clear. The flock—or battalion or legion— evidently had flown off to scavenge breakfast.

He looked down. Whatever had happened, the world continued on its own way. Pedestrians and vehicles scurried this way and that. Someone hurried by on a skateboard. Everything appeared with astonishing clarity although he still hadn't put on his glasses.

He looked up into a shimmering blue sky. An object appeared in the distance. He made out a single pigeon circling overhead. With incredible suddenness, it altered its flight path, flew towards him as if guided by a laser, slowed and alighted on the ledge. Coal black draped its head and neck as if it wore the hood of a medieval executioner. Its body and wings displayed a pure white reminiscent of the unicorn hunted in the famous tapestry.

The pigeon looked at Adonis as if it were about to speak.

Adonis met its gaze in silence. Then he cleared his throat as if preparing to make a statement preempting any possible address by the pigeon. Catching himself at the threshold of absurdity, he put his hand to his mouth.

The pigeon cocked its head as if acknowledging Adonis' predicament.

Adonis dropped his hand and cocked his own head.

The pigeon sprang off the ledge and fluttered in a broad, sweeping circle once, twice, three times before flying off.

Adonis went to the bathroom, pulled off his tee shirt and stood in front of the mirror. An involuntary gasp shot out of his throat. He'd lost weight. A lot of it.

Once, having come down with a terrible flu in high school, he dropped twelve pounds. He knew precisely because each morning his mother made him stand on the scale in her bathroom. Despite his protests, she charted his weight in a notebook. *Numbers tell you all you need to know about people,* she insisted. The weight loss pleased her. She praised him, although he'd done nothing more than take ill. When he regained his appetite, she stuffed him with pasta,

40

homemade bread and three nights in a row pot roast, which his father refused but which he and Apollo devoured. *You look better thinner like your brother*, she told Adonis, *but I'm still your mother*. He regained the weight in a week.

Now it appeared he'd lost more than twelve pounds. Way more. And all since he'd gone to sleep the night before. Which quite possibly hadn't been the night before.

He scratched his head. Had he developed some obscure condition that might prove serious? Even fatal? And why, now that he thought of it, wasn't he hungry? Unless the digital world was playing some fiendish prank, he hadn't eaten for four days and lost a ton of weight. It stood to reason that he'd want breakfast. He didn't. Maybe he'd find time to pick up coffee and a pastry on the way to the Museum. For Anna, too. He bit his lower lip. What might Anna be thinking? Obviously, he hadn't alerted her that he would go missing. Was she worried? He frowned. Did asking such a question represent an assumption about her? About *them*? Was there a *them*?

He reached for his razor and peered into the mirror. His reflection stunned him. Thick, dark stubble carpeted his cheeks, chin and neck. He ran a hand across them. His palm and fingers felt as if they stroked a wire brush. Fearing doing a half-assed job, he decided to skip the shave. That would also save time. Besides, he apparently *had* been sick. What could the Curator in Charge possibly say?

Clutching at his belt buckle, Adonis noticed the elevator still bearing the *Out of Service* sign and began a careful descent of the stairs. He had the odd feeling he could leap down the steps two or even three at a time. One obstacle presented itself. His khakis threatened to fall around his hips. He'd used the Swiss army knife given him by his father for his birthday during his freshman year in high school to bore a new hole in his belt. A safety pin—what were the odds of finding that in his nightstand drawer?—took in the waist of his shorts. His button-down, like his tee shirt, billowed like a ship's sail. His shoes, on the other hand, seemed snug.

Half a flight above the lobby, he spotted the Building Manager. She held a broom with a yellow handle in one hand, a matching yellow plastic dustpan in the other. A brown paper grocery bag squatted in front of her. "Who the hell are you?" she barked.

"Licht," he replied. "Three-oh-two."

Her eyes widened. "The pigeon man? What the hell... What happened to you?"

"I've been sick."

She pointed to the grocery bag. "Broken beer bottles. Wasn't you, was it?"

Adonis halted with two steps to go.

She ran her tongue across her upper teeth. "No. I guess not."

Abandoning prudence, Adonis skipped down the last two steps.

"You maybe want to see a doctor," she said. "What with the weight you've lost."

He placed his free hand over his stomach.

She picked up the bag. "They say bad stuff's been going around. The bugs these days... At least it's the first day of spring. That should be the end of it."

Adonis offered a smile. "About the pigeons."

Choruses of triumph rang out from ledges and windowsills. White splatters marred the sidewalk. Pedestrians sidestepped while looking up warily as if fearing the approach of bombers sent by a hostile nation.

Adonis strolled untouched, coffee and pastries tucked into a cardboard tray. Nearing Anna's alley, he stopped. A police car and a fire department emergency vehicle stood at the entry. He joined a small knot of onlookers observing two uniformed policemen, each wearing blue disposable gloves. The officers spoke softly to a thin man in a military-surplus camouflage jacket and jeans torn at both knees. The man sat on the asphalt propped up by one of the alley's walls. He held his hands behind his back. They appeared to be cuffed or tied. His legs shot straight out and crossed at the ankles.

Adonis looked for Anna but didn't see her.

An older man—perhaps a store clerk or a city employee on his way to work—motioned towards the emergency vehicle where a paramedic applied a bandage over the eye of a man in a gray suit. "Knocked down," he said. He swung his arm towards the thin man as if was testifying in a courtroom. "That guy. Clocked the other guy."

"Why?" Adonis asked. He regretting asking the question, which made him appear naïve.

The man shrugged. "All I know is, he clocks the guy. I was across the street. I saw. Cops saw, too. Cops were coming out of the deli a couple doors down. Lots of cops, they go there for breakfast. Coffee. This guy clocks that guy in plain sight. Didn't even try to run."

Adonis nodded as much in relief as in understanding, although he'd never been the victim of a violent act. A year earlier, someone broke into the lobby of his building and stole a bicycle. That was as close as he'd ever come. Why he'd been spared, he had no idea. He hoped he didn't look like an easy target. Thinking about it now, he supposed in some ways he did. Not like Apollo.

Adonis nodded his thanks to the older man and detoured towards the pocket park a block away.

He found Anna sitting on an old bench with green wooden slats. A dozen or more people had carved initials or symbols into it. Some people called it folk art. He held educated doubts.

He sat then stood again. Would Anna recognize him? Would he frighten her? Taking care, he placed one of the coffees at her side. Then he set down the pastry—a crumb cake of which he was particularly fond.

Anna's eyes twinkled.

"I hope you weren't worried," he said. He felt foolish even as the words left his mouth. Why would Anna feel anything for him? Yet he believed she did. *Wanted* to believe she did. "I was sick. I slept the last four days." He touched the fingertips of his hand to his chest. "And now..."

The twinkle in Anna's eyes faded. Her lids descended just short of closing.

Adonis took her response for concern. Or had she signaled that his illness, the weight loss and the change in his appearance were *not* her concern? For that matter, she could just as well have drifted off into one or another reverie. Still, he refused to sell her short. "I'm better though," he said. "Actually, I feel good." He touched his free hand to his cheek. "Actually, I feel better than good."

Anna's eyelids rose. The twinkle returned.

Fred, the Curatorial Assistant with whom Adonis had worked on the Norbertus provenance, stared as if he were studying a painting. "Maybe you were sick," he said, "but you don't look it now. You don't look like you, either. Well, maybe, but still way different. Like if you had a good-looking brother."

"I do," said Adonis.

"Like him," Fred said. He beckoned with his right hand. Adonis pushed his slice of crumb cake across the desk.

"I only asked for a piece."

"I'm not really hungry."

Fred lifted the cake to his mouth.

"Can I ask you something?" said Adonis.

Fred, crumbs clinging to his shirt and scattered on his side of the desk, nodded.

"Dr. Gelderode... What did she say about my being out of the office so long?"

Fred swallowed and gave the thumbs-up sign. Then he guzzled the last of the mocha with whipped cream he'd brought up from the basement café. "Her Highness, Queen Mary-Louise? I'm not sure. You know how it is when you're occupied with doing your own work and someone else's. Anyway, why should she? Say anything. You called Amy on Monday and said you probably wouldn't be back until Friday. You're a day early."

Adonis arched an eyebrow. "The two of you are on a first-name basis now?"

"Me and Amy? The department admin Amy?"

"Dr. Gelderode."

Fred grinned. "When she's not around, sure. We're all on the same team, right?"

"Only Dr. Gelderode is the department's Curator in Charge."

"Not for long. The woman has ambition. Hell, she's a shark. Think Lady Macbeth. Mary-Louise has smarts, obviously. Also obviously, a body that won't quit. She's not all that much older than we are, and look at where she is. Tyler Severinsen... that's *Dr.* Severinsen to you... better watch out for his job. Same with Hunter Kirk."

"The Chief Curator and the Director? I don't think they're frightened."

Fred licked the remains of chocolate from the cup's inner edge. "If it'll make you feel better, you can call me Mr. del Campo." He tossed the empty in the general direction of their shared wastebasket. It bounced off the rim and back towards his chair.

"In school," said Adonis, "you were probably as good at basketball as me."

Fred bent forward, reached for the cup, took a step back and shot it into the basket. "All I'm saying is, the important people around here all go by a title or a last name."

"Yes, I get that."

"Know why?"

"They're our bosses."

Fred rolled his eyes. "To keep us peons in our place. Put down us brown people."

"I'm not brown."

Fred waved his hand as if he was swatting at a fly. "Us Latinos. Not *you* people. All I'm saying is, why can't Fred or Adonis go into Mary-Louise's office sometime and say, 'Mary-Louise, I'd like to run my hand up your skirt.' Which *you'd* like to do as much as I would."

Adonis wondered if Fred would be happier selling cars or life insurance. Despite his degrees, his temperament seemed less suited to the probity of the museum world than to the one inhabited by Willy Loman. Or was Fred seriously suggesting that Mary-Louise and all the other senior people at the Museum routinely put down brown people? Adonis couldn't see their superiors—socially and politically liberal types—ever doing anything of the sort. Especially given that Hunter Kirk ran the show. At any rate, he did have to concede that Fred knew art. And he made Adonis laugh. "I don't think Dr. Gelderode would appreciate what you just said."

"About the Man... or the Woman... oppressing brown people at this institution?"

"That and the other thing."

"You're right there. We wouldn't get to first base, because we'd have to plead, '*Dr. Gelderode*, may I run my hand up your skirt?' How would *that* work?"

Adonis scratched his chin then rested his hand against his cheek. He wondered if he had a swelling in his jaw although nothing hurt.

"It's just the facts of life," said Fred, "You have to be a ten to bang a ten like Mary-Louise. Or be rich. That's like the same thing."

"You really believe that? That a man would have to be a ten or rich? That you can even rate people?"

Fred winked. "You know who Mary-Louise reminds me of?"

Adonis made no effort to respond.

"Let's get past the Renaissance for a minute. Think of Munch's *Madonna*. Munch, he's not all about *The Scream*. So the Madonnas. Any of them. The long black hair. The tits. The way they look like they want you to jump them. The guy practically painted porn."

"You went to two of the most prestigious private universities in the country, and this is all you think about?"

"I'm just saying. Munch's *Madonna*. Any of them could be a portrait of Mary-Louise. Be honest, doesn't she give off that same vibe? And don't tell me you don't have the same fantasies I do about somehow turning into a ten so you can screw any woman you want."

Not that he'd admit it to Fred, but Adonis had had fantasies along those lines. He still did. He remembered when his biggest fantasy was to be Apollo. Being a ten smoothed over a lot of rough edges. Like holding a get-out-of-jail card. But he'd gotten that out of his system years ago. Or tried. Anyway, who else was *Adonis* Licht supposed to be but himself?

Fred hoisted the remains of the crumb cake.

Adonis tugged on the waist of his khakis.

"So what you need to know," said Fred, "is Mary-Louise is off-campus today through Monday. She didn't say where. Oh, and she *did* tell the staff she hoped you got better soon."

"She could have called me."

"The ruling class talk to people like you and me?"

"She could have called. Admittedly, I was kind of dead to the world so I might not have heard my cell, but she could have. Or somebody could have rung the buzzer to my apartment. Maybe someone did. I don't know. I don't remember anything. I don't remember calling in on Monday." Adonis frowned. "Anyway, no one called."

Fred shrugged. "Look, you called, and Amy gave me the word you'd be back tomorrow. You want chicken soup delivered, call a restaurant. Anyway, if all that weight you dropped is any indication, you weren't just dead to the world, you were nearly dead period." He stretched his arms overhead. "Or maybe you *weren't* sick."

Adonis pressed his hands against the stubble on his cheeks.

Fred smiled. "Maybe you spent the last four days with our friend at the membership desk. *Your* friend. That'll melt the weight off."

Adonis wanted to set Fred straight but couldn't bring himself to confide that Emily had rejected him. Besides, he liked the idea of Fred thinking he could have spent the last four days in bed with her. Or any woman.

❦

Sitting at the foot of his bed that evening, Adonis glanced at a public-television documentary presenting a tour of the Hermitage in St. Petersburg. He followed the camera through the Winter Palace's Twelve-column Hall then turned away. He found it difficult to keep his attention focused on anything. Not that after his first day back at work he felt subject to a relapse. He'd grown stronger as the afternoon wore on. He'd even abandoned his glasses to his desk drawer.

What drew Adonis' attention now were his feet. They'd begun to ache on the walk home. He fantasized Emily massaging them. Then he remembered Fred's advice to thank her for going on the date Saturday night before he fell ill. He'd intended to call her after lunch but forgot as he tried to catch up on the backlog of tasks waiting for him. Remorseful and nervous, he turned the TV down and picked up his cell.

"So hi," Emily said.

Adonis struggled to decipher the tone of her voice.

"Someone said you were sick," she said, responding to Adonis' silence. "The flu or something."

"Someone?"

"Fred? Is that his name? He works with you."

Adonis rubbed his left foot with his free hand. "Fred. He does."

"I was out today. We have this rotating schedule. Everyone gets a Saturday or a Sunday off twice a month. Once a month we get both."

"We're pretty much Monday to Friday except when there's installation work going on. Or occasionally when there's an event and they need me to do a talk or hang around to answer questions. And when a special show's coming up."

"Like the Madonna and Child thing?"

"Like that, sure." He released his foot and wiggled his toes.

"Men usually call after a date. The next day, I mean. Some men."

Adonis bowed his head. "I'm sorry. Really. It's just, I was out of it. I pretty much slept four days straight."

"You slept for four days?"

"It sounds weird, but yes." He paused to figure out what to say next. Then he mentally smacked the heel of his hand against the side of his head. "I enjoyed dinner Saturday night."

"Dinner was nice. It felt a little strange, though. A little... uncomfortable."

"Eating Cuban-Chinese?"

"Not that. I had Moroccan-Thai once. It was good."

"So Cuban-Chinese was okay?"

"It's not... It's... You know how I told you I broke up with a guy?"

Adonis felt a mild stiffness in his lower back. He stood and slowly bent over, one arm extended. His free hand continued downward until it touched the floor. He raised himself as if his fingertips had brushed a live electrical wire.

"Adonis?" Emily asked.

"Sorry. So you broke up with some guy."

"Actually, it wasn't quite like that. He broke up with *me*. Which was okay, I guess. He was kind of an asshole. But women don't heal as quickly as men. Men just don't get it. About relationships. Women want more than a dinner out, although that's a good thing. And sex, sure. That's a good thing, too. But that's not all there is."

Adonis took a breath. "Look, honestly, I feel bad about not calling. And I was thinking maybe we could do something this weekend. There's an opera I can still get tickets to. Or we could go to a movie."

"I'm not sure if I'm ready for a second date. Not that it's you. Besides, this is my whole weekend off. Today and tomorrow, I'm taking vacation days. I'm away. A friend from college is getting married."

"We could have lunch on Monday. Everyone needs to eat."

"Wouldn't that be kind of a date?"

6

onday morning, Adonis lay motionless in bed, eyes closed. A dull ache at the back of his head suggested a hand tightened into a fist. Suddenly, the fist opened. Fingers of pain spread from temple to temple. He groped for his cell. Summoning the will, he opened his eyes. Intense light spilled through the blinds. He blinked. His alarm, he saw, wouldn't go off for another half-hour. He shut his eyes and draped them with his right hand. Outside the window came the sounds of birds chirping. Not cooing. Chirping. He drifted off.

The alarm shook him awake. His hand remained over his eyes, its weight and warmth providing a small measure of relief. He summoned an image of his mother resting her hand lightly on his eyes when as a child he took sick. *I'm sending you healing energy. You'll feel better in no time.* The pain dissipated. Whether the memory had anything to do with it, he didn't know.

Eager to get the new week off to a good start, he showered, shaved and dressed. The last extra hole he'd added to his belt barely kept his khakis up. He put on a fresh shirt. He swam in it. The floor of his closet yielded a pair of sandals, relics from college. He opened the adjustable straps and slipped into them.

He took an apple from a plastic bowl on the small kitchen counter next to the refrigerator, wrapped it in a paper towel and slipped it into his jacket pocket. He could eat while he walked.

Of course, he'd still bring coffee and a pastry to Anna. He'd also buy a coffee for himself. He'd skip the pastry.

Emily led the way as they carried their trays to the far end of the Museum café. A young woman in the cafeteria uniform of white blouse and black slacks cleared the dishes left by two gray-haired matrons standing at the café's wall of windows overlooking the sculpture garden. Their attention focused on a flock of pigeons performing aerobatics the envy of any elite military flying team.

"I was thinking about dessert earlier," Emily said, "but you inspired me."

"To do what?" Adonis asked.

"Pass."

"How did I do that?"

"You're having a salad. Men don't usually eat salads for lunch. Most anyway. Although you could have fooled me the way you ate at the Cuban-Chinese place. Which I liked a lot, by the way. So obviously, you're trying to keep off all that weight you lost."

"I just didn't feel like a sandwich," Adonis said. "Or chips or a soda or anything like that. But *you* can still get dessert."

"God, they make great desserts here, but they're so expensive, even with the employee discount. Anyway, I was just thinking, is all." She turned towards the front of the café. "They write the dessert specials up on the white board on the wall, but you can't make it out from here."

"Warm chocolate cake, rhubarb galette with vanilla ice cream and espresso flan."

She turned back to Adonis. "You can see that without your glasses? Did you get contacts?"

Adonis had no idea how to respond.

She nodded. "Okay, I get it. You never needed glasses. You wore them, but without prescription lenses. You wanted to look more scholarly." She placed her hand on his. "You're ambitious, but you hide it. I bet you want to become Museum Director. Curator in Charge of the Department of Renaissance Art at a minimum."

"I don't think that's likely."

"You never know. That's my philosophy. Anyway, I wish I could lose weight like you did."

"You look fine."

Her eyes narrowed. "Fine? Just fine? You know what the Duchess of Windsor said?"

"Which one?"

"Way back. Wallis Simpson. The one King Edward the whatever...

"The Eighth."

"That one. She said, 'You can never be too rich or too thin.'"

"Well, I haven't been this thin since maybe I was in my mother's womb. Although babies are usually kind of chubby, I think. Anyway, I don't recommend it. The getting sick part. Missing work."

"You have sick days, right?"

"Sure. But if Dr. Gelderode thinks everything went along just fine without me, what then? What if she doesn't see me the way she used to?"

"That," said Emily, "might not be a bad idea. And I'm done with work this afternoon at five."

Straight pins littered the changing room floor where Adonis' old khakis lay in a rumpled heap. His shirt hung like a rag from a hook on the wall. He glanced over his shoulder towards the locked door. Emily waited outside.

She'd insisted on taking him to the department store after work. That seemed odd to say the least, given her confession about being hesitant to date. If he felt uneasy, he conceded that he also felt flattered. And relieved.

His taste in wardrobe matters was sketchy at best. Obviously, he couldn't keep on wearing his old clothes unless he put back most or all the weight he'd lost over the past eight days. Which he now suspected might not happen. At least, not quickly. For whatever reason, he found himself lacking cravings for carbohydrates and sugar. Yet another quick glance in the mirror confirmed what he already knew. Things were different.

Adonis stifled a laugh. Pronounced vertical folds in his tee shirt suggested a fraternity brother at a toga party. He slipped it off then unfastened the safety pin he'd stuck in the waistband of his shorts. They fell to the floor. He chuckled. Wearing only socks and sandals, he could have been taken for a performer in one of those hilarious porn flicks from the nineteen-forties and fifties. He kicked off the sandals and stared at his feet. His socks, manufactured for a range of sizes, were all he had left that fit.

He returned to his reflection in the mirror. This new environment, away from his studio, offered a more objective view of his unanticipated evolution. His forehead seemed broader, his cheekbones higher. He *had* cheekbones! His nose appeared to have straightened and narrowed. His lips struck him as fuller but not too full. And his jaw! His jaw had transitioned to square and prominent without turning him into a caricature.

Adonis took a step back. He easily could be gawking at a distant relative bearing a loose family resemblance defiant of an obvious connection. Moreover, the unfamiliar face might even be considered handsome. Of greater certainty, his shoulders had broadened. He could only describe his chest as muscular. And miracle of miracles, his love handles had melted away. All of which posed a serious question: How did the man in the mirror relate to the man who studied him?

The man outside the mirror carried identification declaring him to be Adonis Licht, although the photos on his driver's license and Museum ID had been rendered obsolete. Of critical importance, the man outside the mirror possessed all of Adonis Licht's memories, could summon all of Adonis Licht's knowledge. No matter how great his external transformation, Adonis felt unchanged *inside*. What people would make of the reflection in the mirror remained to be seen. What concerned him more was what the man outside the mirror, the *real* Adonis, would make of all this.

"And they say women take their time getting dressed," Emily called.

"A minute," said Adonis. He put on a new tee shirt and shorts then a long-sleeve casual shirt. The grid pattern of white lines defined half-inch squares on a navy-blue background. He thought the design might make him look a little less uptight at work while still showing respect for the position he held. After buttoning the cuffs, he slipped into a new pair of khakis.

"You may be changing everything I thought I knew about men," Emily said.

Adonis buckled his new belt.

"Just a joke," she continued. "You're going to look so good, you know? I was thinking, now I can probably show you off. A friend's having people over to her place Saturday night."

Adonis stuck his hand out to brace himself against the wall. Another migraine or whatever it might be seemed to be coming on. Or had Emily staggered him by saying she wanted to go out with him? More than that, introduce him to friends?

"Planning on camping out in there or what?" she asked.

The discomfort passed. "Right out," he said. Still, he felt ill at ease. What was he doing in a department store with a woman he'd dated only once? A woman who'd put him off? Rejected him? The sex part, at any rate. So fine, it had only been their first date. He got that. Now it looked like he just might get his opportunity after all. But a woman going clothes shopping with a man? Wasn't that pushing things in an entirely different direction?

"I could go home," she said.

Adonis emerged from the changing room.

Emily burst out laughing.

"What?" he asked.

She motioned towards a full-length mirror.

Adonis froze. The shirt cuffs rode up his wrists.

"And your khakis."

The khakis weren't near long enough. "They must be mislabeled," he said.

"The shirt *and* the khakis?"

"All these clothes... You know they're made in countries where the workers don't speak English."

She revealed a look of puzzlement. "Men aren't supposed to grow like a decade after college, are they?"

7

The elevator was still out of service the next morning, but Adonis didn't care. He practically leaped down the stairwell, confident that he looked as good as he felt. With Emily's guidance, he'd bought several shirts along with two pairs of khakis, two pairs of slacks, jeans, stylish but comfortable shoes for the office and running shoes for long walks. He thought he might give jogging a try. If he wanted to keep the weight off, he'd have to work at it.

As to being taller, Emily had it right—at least in part. The big weight loss easily could have altered his posture, although that left unexplained the matter of his extended inseam. As to his longer arms and larger hands—his palms had broadened, his fingers lengthened—a mystery remained albeit one perhaps better left unresolved. Adonis saw no point in attracting the attention of what Grandma Sophie used to term *the evil eye*, whose presence she warded off by spitting between her index and middle finger. At any rate, the new Adonis Licht—or that which was new about him—had emerged as a fait accompli. It represented a pretty fair improvement, too. At least, all that involved the *external* Adonis. He'd awakened that morning strengthened in his belief that he remained the same Adonis Licht *inside*. That, however, posed two troubling questions. Did he want to be the same person? And what had the old Adonis made of his life anyway?

At the bottom of the stairs, Adonis found the Building Manager humming as she squatted to clean a corner of the tile floor. "About the pigeons," he said.

"Sounds like Licht three-oh-two," she answered without looking up, intent on dissolving a brownish stain with a stare. "You really like interrupting me every morning?"

Adonis descended the last step.

She looked up and stumbled backwards.

He paused then said, "So the pigeons on the ledge."

She jerked her right hand upward like a marionette in the hands of a child displaying more enthusiasm than skill. "Oh God, my hair. I shouldn't be out here like this. I hope you'll forgive me, Mr. Licht. You look... But you know how women are, I'm sure."

A shoeshine and a smile passed through Adonis' mind.

She pressed her lips together then released them. "I tell you what. There's this high-rated pest control service. I'm sure they can send a man any morning while you're at work. No more pigeons to keep you awake."

"Actually..."

"Nothing's more important than a good night's sleep."

"Well, that's it. I haven't heard the pigeons since I got better. I was sick. Now they're gone."

"Oh," she said. "That explains it. The way you... I mean, you being sick."

"Well, yes. And I'm fine. But it's the pigeons I want to tell you about. It's only been a few days, but hopefully they won't come back."

She clapped her hands together. "There you have it, Mr. Licht. It's only been a few days. Don't kid yourself. They *could* come back. That's pigeons for you. What these pest-control people do is they run some kind of gel along all the ledges. The pigeons think they're snakes. They don't come back for years and years."

"Honestly, you shouldn't have to go to the expense."

"No trouble, Mr. Licht. And don't think of it as an expense. It's an *investment*. An investment in a good tenant. You take care of good tenants, they take care of you, if you know what I mean. Anyway, you'll be at work. No one will disturb you. And José will be sure to wash down the ledge outside your window. The sidewalk, too."

"Thank you, Mrs...."

"Oh, Mr. Licht, please. Margaret."

"Do you think Dr. Gelderode meant what she said at this morning's meeting?" Adonis asked, his concern having shifted from the pigeons to his manager.

"Said what?" Fred mumbled, his attention focused on his cell phone.

"That I look good. All that weight I lost."

Fred offered no response.

Adonis chose not to reveal his disappointment. He honestly felt he'd made a positive impression on Dr. Gelderode. All he asked for was a little reinforcement.

Fred stared at his cell.

Adonis leaned in.

Fred held up his free hand.

Adonis went back to amending notes the two of them had compiled for the Communications Director—background for the announcement of the Norbertus donation at a major media event. Adonis, to his surprise, had been asked to play a small role. He stood and stretched. "Unless I'm interrupting something terribly important, can I ask you a question?"

"Holy shit!" Fred returned in a half-whisper to avoid drawing the attention of the rest of the staff, which included two earnest interns he believed would give eternal thanks to whatever unknown power caused Adonis or Fred or both to fall through a manhole or slip under a garbage truck. Fred held his cell out.

Adonis peered at a man with long blond hair and cheeks lined with creases so deep they appeared to be sewn in place. Hands cuffed behind him, he ducked into a police car as an officer pressed a palm down on his head. Although more into classical music and the American songbook, Adonis recognized the famous rock star. The video cut to a girl, her eyes ringed with black as if she were a panda, bright red lipstick smeared across her mouth. She seemed no older than fifteen.

Fred plucked the phone from Adonis' hand. "You stop at the side of some road miles from nowhere and take a pee. Five minutes later the whole world knows how big your dick is. Or isn't."

"Could you decode that for me?"

"Think metaphor. Think how social media can kill you."

Adonis raised his hand to his mouth. A major celebrity seemed likely to face charges of child molestation and statutory rape, and the world had been alerted by some passerby with a smartphone before any lawyer or spin doctor could make a statement. Privacy was as obsolete as the Greek gods.

"So anyway," said Fred, "I'll look over the notes when you're done. By now we're two of the world's top experts on Norbertus of Hannover."

"There are major *scholars* working on Norbertus."

"Fine, but we're somewhere on the front lines. Given all the time we've put in, we could write a book."

"As far as information goes," Adonis said, "better more than less. That's one of Dr. Gelderode's first principles."

Fred twirled in his chair then leaned forward. "You know she has the hots for Clark Merrill."

"The Clark Merrill who's donating the Norbertus?"

"The Clark Merrill who sits on the Board of Trustees of this acclaimed institution and the boards of a dozen of the country's biggest corporations and nonprofits." He gazed over Adonis' shoulder then back. "Remember the Christmas gala?"

"*Holiday* Gala. You can't do Christmas anymore."

"Probably why we had a twenty-foot tree in the lobby. Anyway, trust me. I saw the two of them talking."

"Why *wouldn't* they be talking?"

"I'm talking the *way* they were talking." Fred shook his head. "Jesus, how do you expect to get anywhere if you can't see past the fifteenth and sixteenth centuries?" He stood. "I'm going to the café for a refill. Get you anything?"

"No thanks."

Fred pumped his right fist into the air. "So *that's* it. You're on some major diet, right? Marine Corp or Navy SEALS or something like that."

"No. I'd just rather hold off until lunch."

"Suit yourself."

Adonis waited until Fred left then turned back to his laptop. A moment later, the screen went fuzzy. Pain raked the backs of his eyes as if sandpaper brushed across his optic nerves. He had no idea how soon Fred would return and no idea what to do when he did. Nor did he want anyone else to see him suffering.

His jaw clenched, Adonis gripped the armrests of his chair and pushed himself to his feet. Taking short, shallow breaths, he walked slowly towards the staff men's room, steadying himself against cubicles then along the wall in the hallway. He pushed on the bathroom door. It resisted. It might as well have been one of the massive bronze doors Ghiberti designed for Il Duomo in Florence. He pushed harder. It yielded. He stumbled into an empty stall and locked the door.

Shutting his eyes, Adonis forced himself to engage in his mother's yoga breathing. Alternating nostrils, he counted backward from one hundred. By fifty, the pain had diminished significantly. By zero it was all but gone.

On returning to his desk, he found that Fred had come and gone again. A yellow sticky displayed Fred's printing, as precise as a computerized type font. *Running an errand— official business. M-L wants to see you!*

"I didn't embarrass you this morning, did I?" Mary-Louise Gelderode asked.

Adonis fought to keep from staring at her breasts. He was glad her desk separated them so he wouldn't be drawn to her legs. Or more particularly, her thighs. Not that he was a gawker. But most men couldn't help it. They were subject to their DNA or hormones or whatever. That, at least, was his rationale. Whether women stared at men, he had no idea. Some did, he supposed. Never at him.

He fixed his gaze on her mouth. Still uncomfortable, he scanned the wall to her left where a shelf displayed a straw handbag with blue trim and a black handle.

She swiveled her head. "The bag? While you were sick I spent a few days in the Bahamas. Recharging. Everyone needs to recharge. They do great straw bags in the Bahamas." She turned back. "Anyway, I asked you a question."

Adonis shifted his focus to her nose. "Embarrass me?"

"I simply wished to compliment you on how good you look after your illness. Different, actually, but good."

"Thank you. That's very kind."

"I mean, you're still the Adonis Licht I hired, right?" The corners of her mouth turned up then dropped. "But I *do* have a concern."

Adonis looked down into his lap then up at her chin.
"You didn't come down with something contagious,
did you?"

"Contagious?"

"I was told you came back to work on Thursday. I
appreciate that. And I'll say it again, you look good. Very
good, really. What I'm wondering is, do you think that your
return might have been a little premature? If you should be
home..."

"I feel fine. Great, actually. I can't imagine I had anything
contagious."

Three delicate furrows appeared in her forehead. "I hope
you don't mind my asking, but as your manager I have an
obvious interest in your wellbeing. You haven't just stopped
eating, have you?"

"I'm eating very well. It's just that I lost a lot of weight,
and I want to keep it off. I'm eating more salads, now. Lots of
fruit, too. There's a pretty good market not too far from where
I live. I'll pick up a grilled chicken breast and vegetables for
dinner tonight. But I'm going to start cooking more."

She leaned forward. The opening of her blouse revealed
the tops of her breasts.

Adonis felt the stirrings of an erection.

"I just want to make sure," she said.

"Really, Dr. Gelderode. I'm fine."

She sat back. "Certainly. Yes. But if you don't mind my
saying so, you look almost elongated. Like an El Greco figure.
Compared to the way you used to look." The fingers of her
right hand, the nails a brilliant red, tapped her desktop.

"I can understand that," he said.

"So tell me, do you have a suit?"

Adonis found himself startled by her abrupt change in
direction. "Yes," he said. "One."

"I mean a suit that fits. That looks decent. *Better* than decent. You've obviously gone shopping. Did you buy a suit?"

"No. I hadn't thought about it."

"Buy one. Take off from work early so you have time to look."

"I have a lot to do today," he said.

"Tomorrow then. Go shopping tomorrow. Get something stylish but still conservative. You'll need a good suit and appropriate dress shirts and ties. And shoes. Men always overlook shoes. I need you to make the right impression."

"I can do that, I guess."

"It's not optional."

He nodded.

She pushed a hair off her forehead. "What I want you to do over the next few months, Adonis, is work on a much higher level. By which I mean associate with important people."

"Shouldn't Fred be doing something like that? He's a year my senior."

"I was going to assign this to Fred... and this is entirely confidential... but now I think you are more appropriate for this task." She placed her left hand on the top of her chest and pulled the opening to her blouse tighter. "It concerns Randolph Bennett, my counterpart at our collaborating museum for the Madonna and Child exhibition. You know who Randolph Bennett is?"

"Of course," said Adonis. "He's pretty much an icon."

"And doesn't he know it! Anyway, Randolph will be coming to town regularly. He wants to see what we're doing for the exhibition and contribute his own thoughts on what he envisions for *his* institution. For starters, he'll be here for the donation event next month."

"We're just completing the notes on Norbertus for the Communications Department."

Mary-Louise waved her hand. "The notes will be perfect, I'm sure. This is an entirely different matter. What I need is someone to be available to Randolph. Someone who can make the right impression while looking after him, so to speak. Meet him at the airport. Accompany him to his hotel. Run to the drug store if he needs something. Randolph Bennett's a treasure and a dear, but he tends to be high maintenance."

"I understand."

"I'm sure you do, Adonis, but I want to be perfectly clear. You'll be getting involved with a whole new class of people. It's important that when these people look at you, they like what they see."

"I'm honored."

"I'm not honoring you, I'm doing business. At my level, careers move along by attracting major donors and supporters. People who can direct their generosity... seven figures, eight... wherever they wish. You may be accompanying Dr. Bennett, as well as myself, to meetings and receptions with these people."

"Like Clark Merrill?" Adonis asked.

"People who travel in important circles. People who take themselves seriously. People *I* take seriously as does Dr. Bennett."

Adonis found his gaze wandering back to her breasts, covered if not concealed. Not, he thought, that she indicated any displeasure. He targeted her nose again.

"So that's it," she said. "Just keep Randolph company and make the right impression." She circled the desk and extended her hand. "Can I count on you?"

Adonis took her hand. It felt warm, almost hot. He regretted having to let it go. An odd thought jostled him. Was Dr. Gelderode sending him a subtle message? Might she be attracted to him? He bit his lip. He was no more a man desired by beautiful women than Anna was a ballerina. "Thank you, Dr. Gelderode," he said. "I'll assist Dr. Bennett any way I can."

She led him to the door. "You know, Adonis, I never noticed it before, which is quite odd. I'm almost embarrassed because I'm a very observant person. In my position, you have to be. But your eyes... They're Prussian blue."

8

As if an unseen Michelangelo or Giambologna had spent the past night sculpting a block of Carrara marble, the bathroom mirror displayed a detailed musculature Adonis had never seen let alone imagined. He couldn't help wondering if what he saw in the mirror and felt when he clasped his biceps or pressed his hand against his stomach might not be an illusion. He found no rational explanation for the four-day slumber from which he awoke like a caterpillar-turned-butterfly emerging from its chrysalis, wings shimmering and ready for flight. Nonetheless, his senses affirmed a new reality. Until and unless he could prove otherwise, he considered it only logical that he take responsibility for his new condition. Granted, the thought of going to a gym left him uncomfortable. But here he was.

Fortunately, the gym fit his budget. A mailer provided a discount for his first six months' membership plus a free consultation with a certified trainer. He would cover the monthly fees by passing on his daily latte and pastry with their copious but empty calories. Shunning lattes alone would pay for the gym. He'd deposit the pastry money into his savings account.

Of course, he'd still bring treats to Anna.

A thought made him shudder. If the radical transformation he'd experienced could take place with such incredible suddenness, he could suffer a reversal just as swiftly. The threat of becoming Cinderella at midnight hovered above his head without extending the obvious advantages Cinderella enjoyed. For all her challenges, Cinderella possessed a measure of perspective given that prior to the royal ball, her Fairy Godmother warned that at the stroke of midnight her gown, carriage and horses all would revert to their former state. Adonis awoke each day shrouded in uncertainty.

Taking a leap of faith, Adonis checked in at the reception desk. In the locker room, he changed slowly.

Back in the reception area, his trainer greeted him. Slim and muscled, he carried a tablet in a gold-and-blue case matching the colors of the gym's logo. He gave Adonis a quick onceover and flashed a grin. "Rob," he said. He extended his hand, his grip firm and assured.

Adonis matched Rob's grip, astonished at the instinctual and effortless nature of his reaction. Then he relaxed and withdrew his hand. He had no desire to engage in the adolescent contest of strength Apollo prized whenever they saw each other.

Rob gestured to the hallway to his right.

Adonis followed him into what loosely resembled a doctor's examining room.

Rob glanced down at his table then up again. "You don't mind taking off your tee shirt, do you?"

Adonis hesitated then complied.

"You a wide receiver back in college or what?" Rob asked. Without waiting for a reply, he said, "So what we'll do is talk a bit about your goals. More strength? Flexibility? Maybe you're a runner or a cyclist now? Triathlete, huh? We'll increase your endurance. Anyway, first we'll do a few simple tests. Then I'll suggest a workout regimen. Having a personal trainer, that makes all the difference. You know how that goes." He made a note on his tablet. "You just move to the city?"

Adonis found the question odd. "No," he replied.

Rob's face indicated a low level of confusion. It passed like an isolated cloud gliding across an otherwise blue sky. "So how come you left your old gym?"

Adonis couldn't imagine himself saying, *That was five years ago and I never put much into my workouts the few times I went and anyway it just happened that I woke up one morning and this is pretty much what I looked like although I never looked remotely like this before and now every morning when I look in the mirror I seem to be in even better shape but I think a gym is a good idea anyway.* Still, he had to say something. "This place is closer to where I work. It'll be easier to come by during lunch or after I get off. Or mornings. Mornings probably."

Rob nodded. "Mornings. Definitely the best. We open at five. I'm here. You want to keep your regimen going. No excuses about being distracted during work or after. Although a guy like you comes to the gym motivated. Like you've got a pretty good six-pack there, but we can add a bit more muscle and definition. Obviously, you had a pretty good trainer at your old gym. But before we do some tests, can I ask you a question?"

Adonis felt the last of his unease drift away like steam rising from a fresh-brewed espresso. Rob could ask all the questions he wanted. Adonis could answer however he wished. The way Rob looked at him—the way the receptionist had looked at him and the woman in the shop and everyone at the Museum over the past week—he couldn't help feeling that people would believe whatever he said. "Sure. Ask away."

"Your name. Adonis. You putting us on?"

"Beautiful," said the associate, examining the gray-blue wool suit Adonis wore out of the dressing room. "Brings out the blue in your eyes."

Adonis studied his image in the three-way mirror. He wasn't born yesterday—although in a way, he was. Associates always found ways to flatter buyers. Or maybe the man was a consultant. An advisor? Forget Willy Loman. The term *salesman* had become a pejorative. Still, the suit *did* look good on him.

"This label is designed for athletic men like you," said the associate. He cuffed Adonis lightly on the arm. His eyebrows shot up. "We'll only have to make a few minor alterations. Usually, our tailor shop is backed up, but for you, I'll fast-track it. Day after tomorrow. That's a promise. So let's look at shirts and ties. And I'll take you over to the shoe department."

A block from the department store, second thoughts about his purchases floated away like soap bubbles. The suit *would* look great on him. It would create an entirely different—what was the word he was looking for? Persona. He'd make the impression Mary-Louise required. He scratched his chin. He'd always thought about her as Dr. Gelderode.

His thoughts turned to Emily. When she saw him in the suit—although he had no idea when she'd have the opportunity—she'd be beside herself. He hadn't taken her along because he thought he could handle the task by himself. More to the point, they weren't a couple. They'd only just started dating. Emily's accompanying him to buy a suit seemed far too intimate.

Not that he wanted to stop seeing her. And yes, he still wanted to go to bed with her. But that was sex. It would happen. The kiss when he dropped her off at her place the night before—their tongues locking like dogs in heat—had sent a message. They ate steak frites at a small French bistro. Adonis left most of the potatoes untouched. Emily took them home. She also insisted on splitting the check since he'd bought the symphony tickets. She wasn't much into classical music, but she agreed to give it a try. He could have worn the suit to the symphony, but that seemed overkill given the seats he could afford. Besides, he preferred to dress casually. Although now it seemed that his new responsibilities would require additional upgrades to his wardrobe.

They'd scheduled another date for Saturday night. That, Adonis figured, would tell the tale. He thought he understood Emily's frame of mind. Some guy had broken up with her a few months earlier, and she still felt the pain. Still, he wondered how anyone could keep carrying around a wound like that. Refuse to let it heal. In fairness, he supposed he still bore wounds inflicted by his mother and Apollo. His father might have hurt him on occasion but more in line with what Catholics called sins of omission rather than commission. He took a deep breath. It was wrong to think badly of the dead.

Two blocks on, Adonis decided to take a detour. The two shopping bags he carried, one with shirts and ties, the other with shoes, were light. Practically weightless. Even considering the lingering remnant of afternoon light, he had time to make dinner before settling in with that new novel about the Borgias. Added to that, he'd kept his horizons too close after moving to the city. A slight change in route would take him to streets he'd overlooked and to which he might wish to return.

Moments later, he entered a neighborhood combining the commonplace with the exotic. The ground floors of apartment buildings much like his revealed a South Asian grocery store, a Thai restaurant, a Russian deli, a shop selling Chinese medicinal herbs. Light from the setting sun glinted off windows as men and women scurried home from work or ran errands at a bakery, a dry cleaner, a pharmacy. Outside a bar, a middle-aged couple engaged in animated conversation. Across the street, two men of indistinguishable age slumped against a black iron lamppost. An undulating haze of cigarette smoke floated above their heads.

The not-unfamiliar flapping of wings captured Adonis' attention. Half-a-dozen pigeons swirled overhead. Even as he stepped under the awning of a liquor store, he chastised himself. What were the odds of again being hit by pigeon shit? Conversely, what about his life could he now classify as normal? Hesitant to step away, he shifted his attention to the store's plate-glass windows. Posters displayed beautiful women, nines and tens, exhibiting long, thick hair—mostly blonde—and large breasts. Several posters featured men, also nines and tens, dressed in tuxedos or spandex workout shirts that emphasized pronounced pectoral muscles and biceps. Each model held up a snifter of this brandy or a bottle of that beer.

Determined to continue his adventure, Adonis stepped away. The sidewalk ahead stopped him. Someone had chalked the outline a human body. One leg extended straight from the torso. The other bent at the knee. The arms pointed in opposite directions, one up, the other down. He thought he might be viewing a street artist's tribute to Keith Haring's work in the 'eighties. Not that Adonis believed Haring to have been all that original. At one time or another, every child placed a hand on a sheet of paper and traced its outline in pencil or beseeched a friend to sprawl on a playground's asphalt surface so that he—or she—might render a chalked silhouette to participate in the ageless delight of replicating the human form.

Uneasy but unable to withdraw his eyes, Adonis studied the outline. Perhaps it paid homage to the movies and TV shows in which such a basic drawing delineated the place where a homicide victim fell. He wondered if police did that given that chalking around a body might risk contaminating a murder scene. Still, producing such an outline as this one was simple enough. It required only that a man of roughly his own size endure a moment of immobility as sensitive flesh rested on unyielding concrete. He considered as well that the silhouette easily could have been his own.

Adonis raised a fist to his lips. What if the outline represented a more chilling option? It might serve as a memorial to someone who had recently died—been murdered—right where he stood. He reminded himself that such a scenario represented pure conjecture. Perhaps being in an unfamiliar neighborhood as evening fell had unnerved him. Still, no matter how disquieting, the outline called to him. How could it not? He was a Curatorial Assistant at one of the nation's preeminent museums. Understanding and explicating art of any kind went beyond his professional duties. It created the passion in his life.

The sun dipped below the rooflines. Streetlights flickered on.

Adonis continued to stare as men and women walked past without slowing. He wondered if he had been sent a sign. Not that he believed in signs and portents. Still, he could not dismiss the possibility that some unfathomable force akin to Penelope nightly undoing the burial shroud she wove for Odysseus' aged father Laertes was now unraveling the warp and woof of the universe.

9

"Here's to Saturday nights!" said Emily. She leaned slightly forward on the desert taupe sofa Adonis had found at a thrift store and reached for the wine he'd opened earlier. A Spanish red. "I can't believe you found this for... What? Eight bucks?"

He gazed at her empty glass. The wine level in his own had decreased no more than half an inch.

She refilled her glass.

"Sorry," he said. "I should have done that."

"Oh god, *I'm* the one who's sorry. I thought, well... It's okay if I pour my own?"

"Sure. You just did." He laughed. He was glad she was drinking. "Am I a bad host?"

"Oh no," she said. "I liked the movie, and now it's kind of nice being here at your place so we can talk without anyone around, if you know what I mean." She held the bottle out.

He shook his head.

"Really? You're giving up wine? Is that part of your diet?"

"I'm not on a diet. I'm just eating differently."

"I guess that's one way of putting it. But really, eating isn't the same thing as drinking. Anyway, it's working for you. I mean, wow. I've never seen anyone change so fast. Like the way Clark Kent ducks into an alley and out comes Superman." She pressed her lips together as if she'd said

75

something she regretted. "What I mean is, it was like, you were sick and then you were okay, only way better than okay." She closed her eyes. "This wine is definitely going to my head." Her eyelids leaped up with unexpected force. "The thing about good wine is, you end up drinking way more than you should and doing things you weren't thinking you'd do. Unless maybe you *were* thinking of doing them. At least, *now* you are."

"Wine can do that," Adonis said. He wondered if she'd brought condoms in her purse. It didn't matter. He kept several in the drawer of his nightstand.

"And *you* can do anything you want," she said. "I mean, being this is your apartment."

Adonis took a deep breath. A good night was about to become a great night. But he didn't want to make himself appear more than what he was. He held his arms out. "It's just a studio."

"But it's all *yours*. If I had a guy over at *my* place, I'd have to make arrangements with my roommates." She made a face. "Women get so territorial."

"Well, *my* problem's always been just finding women. Or a woman." Adonis rebuked himself for making such a lame confession.

Emily took a long sip of wine suggesting that she was weighing her options then leaned closer. "Don't sell yourself short. You were a very nice guy before whatever it was you came down with. I'm sure lots of women wanted to get to know you. But now..." She took another sip of wine. "Wow, this *is* going to my head." She placed her free hand on Adonis' thigh.

Adonis felt the stirrings of an erection.

She stared into his eyes.

"But that relationship you're getting over," he said. He clenched his jaw. Could he have said anything more stupid? Was he getting laid or not?

She squeezed his thigh then slid her hand higher.

Adonis froze. What the hell was wrong with him? He'd almost turned Emily off. Now, he was sitting here immobile when he should be leading her to the bed without another word. Ripping her clothes off on the way. Tossing her onto the sheets. Making her scream or cry or whatever she liked to do when she came.

Then two unexpected questions assailed him. Couldn't he do better than Emily? Was he selling himself short?

"Jesus," she said. "You're soft."

10

The bellman motioned Randolph Bennett and Adonis inside, wheeled in Randolph Bennett's suitcase then gestured towards the room's heating and air-conditioning controls.

Randolph Bennett waved his hand. "You are very kind, but I can handle everything from here." He smiled at Adonis while handing the bellman a tip. "Or at least this bright young man can."

The bellman glanced at Adonis, nodded and left the room.

"I could have brought your suitcase up, Dr. Bennett," said Adonis.

"And contributed to the unemployment of another American worker? Didn't you have an election about that? No, one maintains one's responsibilities to the greater good. My father served as general manager at several of London's finest hotels. He was quite protective of the people on his staffs. Doubtless his attitude had its origins in his rather modest upbringing. While one might not suspect it, he voted Labour election after election. Anyway, you probably don't remember, but once upon a time suitcases didn't have wheels."

"I'm not sure if I do, sir. And I hope you like your room."

"*Randolph*, please. We are, while not contemporaries, associates. And the room is lovely. When I'm in the city, I always stay at this hotel and occupy this room or one just like it. Regrettably, the powers that be refuse me a suite, although I grant that suites at a hotel of this caliber are quite dear." He sat on the bed and patted the brocade duvet cover.

Adonis stepped towards the chair in the corner and sat. "I just want to let you know again that if there's anything you need, I'm here for you. The Museum is delighted that you're visiting us. Me, too. I read your book."

"The one I wrote before coming to America or the one after?" Randolph Bennett held up his hand. "No matter. But do be aware, Adonis, that you hardly strike me as a sycophant. I trust you'll say nothing to change my opinion."

"No, sir."

"Randolph. At least in private. I know how fussy Hunter... Dr. Kirk... can get about these things. But don't misunderstand. He's one of the finest museum directors in the world."

Adonis nodded. "Randolph."

"Better. And now, let's get down to business, Adonis. It's eight-thirty, and I haven't eaten all day. I'm going to ring room service. I'd be quite pleased if you joined me."

"Actually, I had dinner before I went to the airport."

"Dinner? At what hour was that? You hardly strike me as a senior citizen. Or perhaps it was a late lunch?"

Adonis stood. "I really don't want to keep you."

"A glass of wine then? Surely a glass of wine."

"I'd love to," said Adonis, "but I have a very early morning. I go to the gym."

Randolph Bennett stood and placed his hand on Adonis' arm. "And your efforts appear quite successful." He squeezed Adonis' shoulder. "Really, I couldn't be happier to have your assistance. Off to bed with you." He gave Adonis' shoulder a second squeeze.

"While I'm getting a second cup, may I get you coffee, Adonis?" Mary-Louise asked. "We still have important business to discuss this morning. Or have you really given it up?" She scanned the faces at the conference room table. "Which we should all probably do if we want to look as good as Adonis, but we won't."

Hunter Kirk rested a large hand on the table. It blended with the teak surface. "Give up coffee? What are you thinking, woman?"

Mary-Louise smiled. Her eyes revealed a lingering glow of self-satisfaction. Along with the Museum's Communications Director, Lenore Josephson, she had spent the past forty-five minutes detailing the event at which Clark Merrill would donate *The Madonna of the Heavenly Palace*. Several hundred important guests, including the Museum's biggest donors, would attend. The media would come out in force.

On the verge of stammering, Adonis acquiesced. Refusals of meals or drinks or even coffee risked prompting the senior staff—Dr. Bennett, no less—to think him standoffish. One cup would pose no harm. Besides, Mary-Louise Gelderode getting coffee for *him*? Of course, she might only be seeking to impress Randolph Bennett, defining herself as an egalitarian, a woman of the people.

"Milk?" she asked. "We have low-fat."

"Yes, thank you, Dr. Gelderode."

"You can dispense with the formalities," said Hunter Kirk. "You've crashed the inner circle, Adonis. That puts you on a first-name basis with everyone around this table. At least, while you're here in this room." He turned to Amy Levine-Franklin, the department Admin. "Isn't that right, Amy?"

"Yes, sir," she said.

He winked at Adonis. "Call me Hunter, son."

Randolph Bennett turned towards Adonis. "It's official then. But do not even *think* of calling me Randy."

Tyler Severinsen, the Chief Curator, made a show of laughing.

Randolph Bennett—Randolph now—grinned at Adonis from across the table. "I could tell you stories about Tyler, but I remain the soul of discretion." He leaned forward. "Maintain the right public face," he said in a carefully modulated stage whisper, "and whatever you do will never imperil you or your career."

"What Randolph in his best British manner means," said Tyler Severinsen, "is cover your ass or something's going to take a big chunk out of it."

Although the banter took Adonis by surprise, he managed a grin. He most often experienced an almost palpable reserve at meetings with senior staff and visitors. Inevitably, he went back to his desk feeling as if he'd been sucked into an emotional black hole. Obviously, he stood on the brink of a new world.

Mary-Louise placed coffee in front of Adonis then circled the table to sit at the end opposite Hunter Kirk.

Adonis' eyes followed her brief journey. Responding to an awkward measure of self-consciousness, they drifted down to his hands in his lap. To his left and right, Lenore Josephson and Amy Levine-Franklin held their own hands poised above their laptops.

Hunter Kirk brought Adonis back to the task at hand. "So anyway, Mary-Louise," he said, "there's something else you wanted to discuss?"

Mary-Louise nodded.

Amy passed out crimson folders.

"First," said Mary-Louise, "I want to leave everyone with these major communications points Adonis and Lenore put together. Over the past decade... the last several years particularly... the art world has rediscovered Norbertus of Hannover."

"What Mary-Louise means," said Tyler Severinsen, "is that Norbertus is hot."

Lenore Josephson opened her copy of the briefing. "I've included a list of sale and auction prices over the last five years for works by other noted artists of the period, particularly in the range of *The Madonna of the Heavenly Palace,* and one other Norbertus. Of course, we're not talking about *Picasso's Women of Algiers*, which went for a hundred seventy-nine million at Christie's. That's something else completely."

"If our Norbertus had an appraised value like that," said Hunter Kirk, "you'd be out of a job, Lenore. We just wouldn't need you."

"Thirty-five million dollars isn't chopped liver," said Lenore Josephson. "There's a ring to anything worth eight figures. At any rate, we want to shine a light on Mr. Merrill's generosity and the importance of this painting to the Museum. There's also a detailed backgrounder on Norbertus' life along with a narrative on *The Madonna of the Heavenly Palace*. Adonis wrote it."

"The Greek god of Renaissance art," said Randolph Bennett.

Soft chuckles rose like bubbles in a hot tub.

"So that's it then," said Hunter Kirk.

Mary-Louise held up her index finger. "As I previously mentioned to Tyler, I'm proposing that we enlarge the size of the gallery devoted to Norbertus' life and the back-story regarding his Madonna. We're in the final stages of planning the exhibition, and we need to commit now."

"Tyler, do we need the space?" asked Hunter Kirk. "Do we *have* it?"

"We can make an adjustment, Hunter. There *is* a back-story. And it seems like every day one scholar or another unearths something new." He motioned towards Randolph Bennett. "Randolph's people are doing quite a bit of research in coordination with Mary-Louise's people."

"With Adonis," said Mary-Louise. "Others in the department are pitching in, of course. But following Randolph's suggestion, from our end this is Adonis' baby."

Hunter Kirk ran his right hand over his beard then glanced at his watch. "Go run with it, Adonis," he said. "Tell us what we need to know so we'll all be on the same page."

Adonis' cheeks flushed. He hadn't expected that Hunter Kirk would call on him. Just as suddenly, his cheeks cooled. An unanticipated calm enveloped him. He'd come to the meeting prepared just in case. He approached Mary-Louise's chair.

Mary-Louise brought up a projection of one of the two known portraits of Norbertus. One was a work in oil by a little-known known Dutch painter, possibly an apprentice to Norbertus in his latter days, the other a pen-and-ink sketch by Norbertus himself.

"On a scale of one to ten," said Tyler Severinsen, "a four. A five if you want to cut Norbertus a little slack." He glanced around the table. "Not the art. The man."

Adonis never imagined rating Norbertus' looks but set the matter aside. He buttoned his suit coat. "As with most artists," he said, "there's an intriguing story behind Norbertus. It's about religious persecution, first in Italy then in Holland."

Hunter Kirk made no response.

"Not to be cynical or flip," said Adonis, "but persecution... religious intolerance and all that... sells. I know that Mary-Louise and Lenore agree. And there may be something else. We're looking into it."

Hunter Kirk laid his right hand over his watch. "Go on," he said.

Adonis laid out the basics. Norbertus was born in 1550 in Hannover, a principal city of the Protestant northern German states. He attended school until age twelve then worked with his father, a silversmith who achieved modest success despite suspicions that he was a secret Catholic. Within two years, Norbertus was creating pieces of significant merit for the shop's patrons. Two of those pieces were now on display in Berlin. The origins of Norbertus' painting were unclear, but in 1569, with his father's encouragement and limited financial support, he went to study in Rome.

Adonis paused to gauge the level of his audience's attention and registered his own astonishment. Senior staff seemed determined to hear what they could read in the report they'd been given. More, they hunched forward, intent on every word.

"So what happens is," Adonis continued, "within a year, Norbertus finds a benefactor. It's Cardinal Baldassare Giordano. Later he becomes a candidate for Pope."

Roman tongues clacked. The Cardinal's interest in the nominally Protestant Norbertus brought hushed rebukes in some quarters of the Vatican. Important corners. Nonetheless, Norbertus kept at his studies and sold several paintings, albeit for insignificant sums. In March 1576, most of his work, stored in the palace of Cardinal Giordano, perished in a fire. Rumor implicated Pope Gregory XVIII, who reformed Europe's calendar six years later. In May, Norbertus fled to Hannover, which coincided with his father taking ill. Norbertus managed his father's shop and remained at that post following his father's death from an infection after the removal of several teeth. Employing apprentices, Norbertus devoted the bulk of his time to painting. He experienced as little commercial success in Hannover as in Rome.

"Scholars," Adonis said, "suggest that Norbertus' failure at home resulted from Protestant hostility to his relationship with a prince of the detested Church."

Hostility mounted. In 1581, a Protestant mob torched Norbertus' studio. Norbertus fled to Amsterdam where he found refuge with a wealthy Catholic merchant in what had become an extraordinarily tolerant city.

"Very nice," said Hunter Kirk. "We'll get a good deal of mileage out of this. Lenore's our Rumpelstiltskin spinning straw into gold. Bottom line, this has all been quite engaging. But Adonis, you mentioned something more about Norbertus before you started. Another back-story."

Adonis looked at Mary-Louise then back at Hunter Kirk. "We should really focus on the painting itself right now. Norbertus paints *The Madonna of the Heavenly Palace* in Amsterdam in 1582. That's a year before he dies. Tuberculosis probably. He's thirty-three. When he dies." Adonis paused. While this detail was familiar, he'd only now registered the fact that Norbertus died so close to his own age.

Mary-Louise brought up an image of the painting. "Mr. Merrill had it shot," she said.

Adonis pointed to Mary's crimson cloak. "In most paintings," he explained, "she wears a cloak of blue. Sometimes black. She might wear a crimson or red garment underneath, but her cloak is usually blue to signify royalty. The Queen of Heaven."

"And the significance of the crimson cloak?" asked Hunter Kirk.

"Well, there's a suggestion of a link or bond with Cardinal Giordano. Mary's red cloak relates to the red robes of a prince of the Church. And the infant Jesus, he's pointing up not so much to heaven as to a palace floating above a cloud. It's pretty much out of the ordinary in terms of iconography."

"Which means?" asked Hunter Kirk.

"We know that the palace is the Palazzo Giordano, not far from the Vatican. It dates from 1395, and it was rebuilt in 1517. Cardinal Giordano purchased it in 1564. He completed renovations four years later but then he suffered some financial reverses."

"The heavenly palace," Mary-Louise cut in, "symbolizes Christ's mission to offer humanity life after death. A magnificent life people never could have here on earth. Not that the palace is meant to be taken literally. Or maybe it is."

Adonis cleared his throat. "In September 1582, Norbertus mentions the painting in a letter to Giordano. He says he's about to finish it. It's a gift. He'll send it to the Cardinal within a month. The Cardinal will be very pleased."

An English academic discovered the letter in Rome in 1893. It appeared in an obscure volume published by Oxford University a decade later. Nonetheless, *The Madonna of the Heavenly Palace* made its first public appearance only in 1946. The daughter and sole survivor of a Belgian-Jewish family lost in the Holocaust sold three paintings by Norbertus to an art dealer in Brussels. The dealer in turn sold them to a speculator, who despite the ravages brought on by the war bided his time to maximize his potential return on investment. Amsterdam's Rijksmuseum purchased *The Elders* in 1947. The Uffizi Gallery acquired *The Kitchen Maid* in 1949. Since Norbertus was considered a second-tier painter and funds were limited, both brought only modest sums. From 1953 on, *The Madonna of the Heavenly Palace* passed through the hands of a series of collectors. Clark Merrill bought it in 2004.

"The only other Norbertus known to be in private hands," Adonis related, "is purchased at auction by a Russian collector in 2009. He pays eight million Euros. It's assumed to be worth at least twice that now. But that still doesn't bring it up to the valuation of our painting. The Norbertus in the Louvre was appraised last year for nineteen million Euros. It's not as valuable, or as interesting, as ours."

Hunter Kirk looked at Lenore Josephson.

"We've got a good story," she said. "There's a certain reporter who's particularly interested, and I guarantee that the story will be picked up all around the country."

Hunter Kirk rapped the heel of his hand on the table. It shuddered. "Let's get on with it. I expect us to generate impressive numbers with this show. I've made a commitment to the board, not to mention our corporate sponsors. But this religious intolerance angle. Let's be careful."

"Tell me about it," said Randolph Bennett. "We've got Cardinal O'Hare coming to our gala opening. Although who is he to complain? He's never gotten over the Reformation and don't think that doesn't hit home. I *am* Church of England these days. At any rate, I wouldn't be surprised if he starts talking about having Norbertus beatified. Canonized perhaps." He looked at Adonis. "And this other business you mentioned? You don't care to tell us about it this morning?"

Mary-Louise interjected. "It's still not buttoned down, but I expect Adonis will have something for us in a few days."

Randolph Bennett turned to Hunter Kirk. "I don't doubt Adonis will ferret out something advantageous to our purposes. Sherlock Holmes has nothing on our young colleague, I'm sure. Although a small confession. I've never much admired Conan Doyle. I prefer Simenon's Maigret. At any rate, I'll keep my people in close touch with Adonis."

Hunter Kirk looked around the table. "Whatever it takes to educate the public and sell tickets, let's make it happen." He stood and held up his folder. "I'll review this, although it seems like Adonis has covered all the bases." He turned to leave then swung back to face Randolph Bennett. "You're coming to the donation ceremony, of course."

"With bells on."

Hunter Kirk smiled. "Well, I assumed *that*, Randolph." He looked around the table, noted the requisite signals of affirmation then strode out of the conference room.

The remaining participants, less Mary-Louise, followed like ducklings trailing their mother.

Adonis began clearing the table.

"Café staff will handle that," said Mary-Louise.

He put down two sets of cups and saucers.

"I just want to tell you, Adonis," she said, "that you impressed Hunter, and he's not easily impressed." She kissed him on the cheek and left.

Adonis took a triumphant breath. Then a matter of no little significance wriggled forward from the back of his mind. Susan Ricketts, the department's Assistant Curator, hadn't attended the meeting. A revelation followed. He hadn't seen Anna that morning. He'd gone to the gym then straight to work. For that matter, he hadn't visited her the day before. Or, he realized, for the past week. For that matter, it might have been longer.

Slouching more than sitting in Mary-Louise's office that afternoon, Adonis leaned back in his chair, his right leg extended, his suit coat unbuttoned.

Mary-Louise perched on her desk. The hem of her skirt rested well above her knees.

Adonis interpreted her body language as corresponding to his own and signaling a major shift in their relationship. To someone outside the Museum, they likely appeared a man and woman engaging each other with a longstanding familiarity, an intimacy transcending their professional lives.

He recognized that he'd undergone a profound change. Regarding his appearance at any rate. He'd begun to accept it. Still, a major question confronted him: Was his psyche experiencing a corresponding alteration? He'd failed to identify some internal mechanism—an emotional mirror of sorts—to provide even a minimally objective evaluation. Regardless of the agreeable nature displayed to him by people at work and away from the Museum, the matter left him increasingly unsettled. He feared suffering a distortion of the inner self he believed to be good and true despite his obvious cruelty to Emily. He'd never intended to bring her to tears—to offer her only a perfunctory *I'm sorry* as she called a ride service to take her home. But being on the cusp of going to bed with Emily brought him to the stark realization that he'd long acquiesced to limited horizons. It wrested from him the acknowledgement that he *did* fantasize about Mary-Louise. Fred always had been right about that. And yes, he *was* thinking of his department manager as Mary-Louise.

Was he deluding himself that she was thinking of him? He couldn't possibly know. His own thinking remained murky. Surely, most men considered her an object of desire— excepting the Randolph Bennetts of the world. Had he the courage to reveal his attraction? He cautioned himself that his career—his job at least—depended on her.

Responding to an inner voice that spoke without words, he retracted his leg, sat up and dropped his hands into his lap. Despite his small act of discretion, an unbidden warmth crept over him. His hands became aware of the stirrings of an erection. He pressed his legs together. Did Mary-Louise suspect? She *had* to know how men responded to her. How *he* responded to her. Were he a character in a best-selling novel or a Hollywood movie, he'd lock the door and screw her right there on her desk. She'd love it. More, she'd thank him for it.

What poise Adonis displayed when he'd entered the office withered along with his budding erection. He feared that she'd called him in because he'd said something out of line during the meeting that morning. Maybe he'd taken Hunter and Tyler and Randolph and Lenore too much for granted. Perhaps they'd all been putting him on, testing him, anticipating that he would abuse the privilege to address them by their first names and reveal his lack of suitability to join the inner circle.

Mary-Louise smiled as if she intuited his doubts. "You were terrific this morning," she said. "Everyone hung on your every word."

Adonis let loose an inaudible sigh of relief. "Thank you," he said. Yet any thought of addressing her as Mary-Louise vanished. It seemed wiser not to address her by name at all. "I'm glad Dr. Kirk approved the larger gallery space for Norbertus. We're lucky to have the painting donated."

"Not until next week's donor gala when Mr. Merrill signs the papers. And trust me, Adonis, luck had nothing to do with it." She tugged at the hem of her skirt.

It struck Adonis that she knew exactly how that small action would draw his attention.

"Of course," she said, "we'd have raised the funds for the painting if we'd needed to. Hunter and Tyler are masters at extracting every last dollar from major donors."

"I'm sure," said Adonis. He clasped his hands, the fingers intertwined. Then he unclasped them. "May I ask a question?"

Mary-Louise's eyes pierced his like the arrows that martyred St. Sebastian in Mantegna's three paintings.

He hesitated.

"And your question is?" she asked.

"Dr. Ricketts didn't attend the meeting this morning."

"No. She didn't."

"May I ask why?"

Mary-Louise laughed and tossed her hair like a high-school cheerleader encountering the captain of the football team alone in a quiet corner of the cafeteria. "I have a feeling there's no keeping secrets from *you*," she said. "It hasn't been announced, but Susan has taken a wonderful position at a major museum in another city. She'll be with us for another three weeks, but she's out of town for a few days looking for an apartment."

"Will she be here for the donor event?"

"She will, but as a lame duck, only in the background. No hard feelings, of course. I like Susan. I'll miss her. But career comes first."

"I suppose," said Adonis. "That is, yes. I want to build my own career, of course." He left unsaid that he would gladly build it on Susan Ricketts' departure, understanding the folly of being thought of as too eager to ascend to her position. On the other hand, he wanted to assure her that he possessed the necessary ambition required for serious consideration. "Have you selected someone to replace her?" he asked. But as soon the words tumbled out of his mouth, he wished he could gather them up. He'd gone too far. Yet he could no more withdraw his words than a Renaissance infantryman could recall the iron ball he'd just fired from his arquebus.

Mary-Louise sat in the chair next to his and leaned forward.

Adonis registered her perfume. He feared that its fragrance and intensity menaced his judgment.

"I've been speaking with Tyler," she said. "Whoever we recommend, we'll have Hunter's approval."

"I don't doubt it in the least," said Adonis, in part to be agreeable but also to demonstrate that he could uphold his end of the conversation. If this *was* a conversation. And if he was speaking with a minimum of coherence.

"As it happens, Tyler and I have someone in mind. We'll run the matter by Hunter tomorrow." She rested her hand on his. "As for this evening, I'm hoping you have time to join me for a drink."

11

Randolph Bennett accepted a flute of champagne from one of the white-coated waiters crisscrossing the Museum's lobby then turned to Adonis. "Only my second, and I promise to be very careful this evening," he said. "I take it that you, my dear Adonis, as a man dedicated to fitness and good heath obviously will not be drinking at all."

"Maybe when Mr. Merrill signs the painting over to the Museum," said Adonis.

Randolph Bennett raised his glass. "To beauty, truth and all the delights that charm and reward the senses." As he sipped, he turned his head. "I would tell you that I loathe these functions, but I would be dissembling. I adore them. Having made that confession, I must disclose that several people await with whom I absolutely must speak. While I thank you for escorting me to the Museum and do love having you on my arm, I will renew some very useful contacts and make several new ones."

Adonis watched Randolph Bennett slip into the crowd then threaded his way to the side of the general admission desk where Lenore Josephson planned to meet him. Sunlight streamed through the Museum lobby's towering windows, the spring evening reluctant to yield to nightfall. He reflected on the light in the cathedrals he'd visited on several trips to Europe and in train stations, themselves cathedrals in an era whose gods represented science, manufacture and commerce. He remembered a moment during his undergrad semester in Rome as he waited to board a train to Milan. A Brit possessing something of the air of Randolph Bennett commented that cathedrals and train stations bore an uncanny resemblance. Both types of edifice projected an aura of stateliness and met the needs of people just passing through.

Furious motion tugged Adonis back to the present. Men in dark suits and women in cocktail dresses staggered backward and forward, faces tilted upward, hands shielding impeccably styled hair. Adonis spotted the object of their attention—a solitary pigeon, the only guest not in possession of a highly valued invitation. Exclamations of distress rendered inaudible a string quartet playing Haydn.

Staff members rushed to open all the doors.

The pigeon made a final circuit of the lobby then exited with what might have passed for a gesture of contempt.

Guests returned their attention to plucking stuffed mushrooms, shrimp and tiny meatballs from passing silver trays. Small knots of men and women, like schools of fish in a feeding frenzy, skimmed across the marble floor pursuing more substantial delicacies displayed on tables encircling the large glass skylight that peered down into the basement galleries. Other guests emerged from bars tucked behind soaring columns set in rows flanking both sides of the lobby. They clutched drinks with the triumphant demeanor of battle-tested legionnaires flourishing booty.

Camera crews and reporters wove their way among the guests, stopping periodically to interview a well-known captain of industry, attorney, culture maven or socialite.

A hand tapped Adonis' shoulder.

"Permission to speak," said Fred.

"Get real," Adonis replied.

"I couldn't get any *more* real. You're my boss."

"*Mary-Louise* is your boss. And *mine*."

"But Sue Ricketts is like nine-tenths out the door, which is why they assigned her to shadowing the caterer or something like that. We all got the email announcing you as the designated Assistant Curator in Charge."

Adonis shrugged.

Fred snared a meatball. "The way it is, you've risen a major rung above me on the food chain. When you say, 'Run over to the bar and get me a whatever,' I'm supposed to answer, 'Yes, sir, with or without ice.'"

"Bullshit."

"*Now* who needs to get real?"

Adonis spotted Emily near the main entrance. Staff, along with members of the department, had been positioned to take coats to the cloakroom, direct guests to the bars and restrooms, and provide any other assistance.

Emily saw him and turned away.

Fred gestured with his chin towards a nearby cluster of VIPs. Clark Merrill stood at the center. His arm encircled Mary-Louise's waist. "I hear Mrs. Merrill's in Mexico. Or the Caribbean. Bangkok maybe."

"And you know this how?"

"There's this blog."

Adonis focused on Clark Merrill, silver-haired and as slim as an Olympic marathoner. Mrs. Merrill might be only yards away for all he—or Fred—knew. If not, she might be home with the bug that was going around. Although not his bug. If he'd had a bug.

Clark Merrill drew smiles then a burst of laughter from Hunter Kirk and the President of the Museum Board. Next to the President stood a woman wearing an elaborate gold pendant that would have been at home snuggling the bosom of Elizabeth I. Adonis assumed she was the President's wife. Two other couples completed the group. One of the women looked familiar. Adonis finally placed her. The Mayor.

Lenore Josephson approached. She held the hand of an attractive woman with honey-blonde hair.

Adonis took the woman to be about his age. He computed her at an eight. Eight-plus. Not quite up to Mary-Louise but certainly attractive enough. *More* than attractive enough. Pressure built in his chest the way it always did when he met good-looking women.

"Carla," said Lenore, "this is Adonis Licht, Assistant Curator in Charge of the Department of Renaissance Art."

"About-to-be Assistant Curator," said Adonis.

"Approval's a formality," said Lenore. "Adonis is one of our bright, shining young stars. He assembled all the information on Norbertus of Hannover."

"I need another drink," said Fred. He drifted off.

"Carla Parsont," Lenore said, "is covering the event for our favorite newspaper whose reach, they continually inform us, extends from coast to coast and far beyond our shores. I know she'll get some fabulous background from you."

"You must be very important here," said Carla Parsont.

Lenore patted Adonis on the shoulder. "We call him our Greek god of Renaissance art."

Adonis stared at his feet.

"And humble," the reporter said. "Like all the other guests here."

Adonis raised his head and grinned.

Lenore nudged Adonis forward. "He's all yours," she said to the reporter and started across the lobby.

The reporter held up a small digital recorder. "So assuming Greek gods know everything or nearly everything, just how did the Museum wangle this painting... this donation... from Clark Merrill?"

No one, Adonis explained, had wangled anything. Clark Merrill had been a loyal supporter of the Museum for fifteen years and a member of the Board of Trustees for the past decade. "Mary-Louise Gelderode... *Dr.* Gelderode... would be the more appropriate person to ask about that."

"A gift like this must involve major tax considerations," she said.

"Tax considerations. Yes. Gifts to museums usually do. Involve tax considerations. As far as the valuation goes, the Museum hired an independent appraiser. You'd want to speak with Dr. Kirk and Mr. Merrill."

Carla Parsont tilted her head. Thick, honey-blonde hair cascaded over her right shoulder. "Given the build-up I just got from Lenore, I'm thinking you might be more helpful than that."

Adonis swallowed. He considered excusing himself. Then the knot in his chest released, as if they were playing roles in a dated film and someone had slapped his face to bring him around. "Actually, my expertise is in the painting's iconography... the symbolism and all. And the artist. I know Norbertus of Hannover as well as I know myself. Probably better." He cocked his head. "Does that sound odd?"

"Most of us don't know ourselves nearly as well as we think we do."

"Anyway, Dr. Gelderode's going to speak about Norbertus and the painting. And Mr. Merrill, of course. Then we'll witness the signing of the papers transferring *The Madonna of the Heavenly Palace* to the Museum."

"And we'll finally get to see what this whole evening is all about."

Adonis gestured to the easel on a platform to their right. A gray cloth covered the painting.

Carla Parsont lowered her recorder. "Thank you, Mr. Licht."

"Adonis."

"Adonis, you bet. The Greek god and all that." She extended her hand. "Not that I'm blowing you off, but I have a bunch of people to speak with." She reached into her shoulder bag and withdrew a business card. "But if, you know, anything should come up. Anything more specific."

Adonis watched Carla Parsont elbow her way across the lobby like a commuter on a crowded train platform.

His attention shifted to Lenore Josephson escorting a television crew towards Clark Merrill, whose entourage, now including Randolph Bennett, stepped aside.

A female TV producer motioned Clark Merrill to turn to his left then held her thumb up.

Clark Merrill smiled at a male reporter wearing a blazer, jeans and running shoes. A bright light came on.

Adonis discovered Mary-Louise leaning against him. Her lips moved, but he couldn't make out the words.

She touched her throat. "I need you," she said in a voice so soft Adonis had to read her lips. She held up the event program with its list of speakers, pointed to her name and shook her head.

"That's terrible," said Adonis.

She poked her right index finger into his chest.

"But I didn't prepare anything."

Her face contorted.

He nodded.

She kissed him on the cheek and fluttered off.

Adonis contemplated a moment of yoga breathing, but considered it both inappropriate and unflattering to be seen pressing a finger first to one nostril then the other then back again. He settled for a deep mouth breath.

Hunter Kirk leaped onto the platform and took a microphone from its stand. The crowd hushed while TV lights blazed like flares over a battlefield. With polished ease, he welcomed the President of the Board, who expressed his great delight that these distinguished guests could share in another of the Museum's fabled accomplishments. The Mayor followed, saluting the Museum, its benefactors and the city for modeling civic involvement and unsurpassed generosity. Tyler Severinsen commended the considerable effort by Museum staff to find acquisitions befitting one of the nation's—indeed, the *world's*—leading art institutions.

Then Adonis found himself microphone in hand.

He detailed Norbertus' life, his love of the Church despite all difficulties, and his finding a benefactor in Rome to whom he had dedicated *The Madonna of the Heavenly Palace.* His mind operating on dual tracks, he avoided any hint of another story that might paint Norbertus in something of a different light. Research was still in progress. Moreover, when the Museum possessed all the details, Lenore would stage a separate media event. She'd first leak the news to deflect any possible onus from the Museum onto the scholars who had uncovered the matter. Still, he couldn't imagine the discovery making anything but a minor impact in terms of hard news, although it likely would ruffle a few feathers. All things considered, Museum revenue would come out ahead.

Adonis' words and the thoughts concealed behind them concluded, the crowd burst into applause.

Startled, Adonis gathered his wits and nodded to project the requisite humility. Then he handed the microphone to Hunter Kirk.

The applause grew louder.

Hunter Kirk clasped his arm with a hand that could have crushed muscle and broken bone.

Clark Merrill bounded onto the platform. Wrapping an arm around Adonis' shoulders, he took the microphone. "Before we begin the formalities," he said, "I have to confess that nothing I can tell you about Norbertus of Hannover's magnificent work could match the eloquence and power of what we just heard from..." He looked at Adonis.

Adonis whispered in his ear.

Clark Merrill smiled as if he'd concluded a major business deal. "Adonis Licht."

The Building Manager's red hair glistened in the early morning sunlight as if it was on fire. She hoisted aloft her morning newspaper. "Oh my goodness, Mr. Licht. Did you see this about you at the Museum last night?"

Adonis shook his head.

"Really?" she asked.

"I don't get the newspaper," said Adonis. "And I'm just leaving for the gym."

"Well, you should start. Getting the paper, I mean." She held out the front page of the Arts & Living section.

A prominent photo displayed a grinning Clark Merrill holding Adonis in something of a bear hug. He remembered the moment quite clearly. Still, he didn't quite recognize himself.

12

The buzzer in his apartment elevated Adonis' state of apprehension to an even higher level. With only a few minutes warning, he'd been forced to drop his plans to go to the gym following a triumphant Saturday-morning talk on Norbertus delivered to a standing-room-only audience in the Museum's main auditorium. Lips pressed together, he closed his laptop, slipped into his sandals, opened and locked the apartment door, and forced himself down the stairs.

He paused at the bottom step then crossed the lobby and opened the entry door. He hoped that a smile would camouflage his uneasiness.

His mother's narrowed eyes gave the impression of a mugging victim at a police line-up struggling to identify her attacker.

Adonis waited for her to speak.

She seemed, uncharacteristically, at a loss for words.

He considered that she thought him an imposter—a criminal with a vague resemblance to her son engaged in a plot to kidnap her and hold her for ransom. He took the downward arch of her perfectly plucked eyebrows and the inward curl of her lower lip as indications that she envisioned her attorney receiving a phone call demanding a million dollars. Or more. Perhaps substantially more. He gave her a perfunctory hug. His cheek brushed hers.

She stood motionless, as if authenticating his scent.

He dropped his arms.

They rode up in the elevator. The motor strained noisily. She maintained her silence.

He unlocked the door to his apartment.

She hesitated.

"It's the studio I found when I moved here, remember? I guess you've never seen it."

"No need. You come home every year."

"I'm thinking I might look for a bigger place. A one-bedroom."

"Ambitious, aren't you?" she said.

Adonis wished she'd said something like, *It's so good to see you. I miss you, even in my mansion. And you look so wonderful.* But he made no effort to push back. He loved his mother, although he knew that love encompassed more colors than might be found in a painting by Masaccio or Ghirlandaio. Besides, a retort would only make the situation more uncomfortable. He decided to point the conversation in her direction. "You look wonderful, Mother."

"What did you expect? The grieving widow? I got over that the day after we buried your father. My side of the family has always been matter-of-fact about death." She raised a hand to her hair, silver-blonde with a hint of a wave. "Thank God I finally found a hairdresser who understands me." She sat on the sofa, her knees pressed together like magnets.

"Can I get you something to drink, Mother? Something to nibble on?"

"Thank you, no. I ate on the plane. Thank God they still serve meals in first-class, as pedestrian as it is. And I had a piece of fruit in my suite before the hotel limo dropped me off."

"I have to say, you caught me by surprise."

"I *had* to come after your picture appeared in that magazine. Charlotte Gruden saw it. She said, *There's an Adonis Licht who works at the same museum where your Adonis works and I saw his picture. Imagine two men working in the same museum and having the same name that isn't John Smith or something like that.*"

"Actually, there's only one of me."

His mother's expression remained unchanged. "Charlotte brought the magazine over. I must have stared at that photo for fifteen minutes. I said to Charlotte, *Looks nothing like my Adonis. But two Adonis Lichts? I better find out.*"

"Well, I know it sounds weird, but I've been working out a lot. Like Apollo. And I'm eating better. Eating healthy. You're sure I can't get you something?"

She stared. "Since when do you wear contact lenses?"

"I don't."

"Your eyes. Why are they blue? And such a bright blue?"

"Maybe they were gray-blue when I was younger but no one noticed. I think eyes sometimes change when you get older. Like the way hair color changes."

"Children go from towhead to brunette. That's common. Brunette to red or blonde? That's unnatural. For men at any rate."

"Well, I'm still me. Adonis. *Your* Adonis."

"Your voice... It's the voice of my Adonis, yes. The rest of you... I told Charlotte there had to be a rational explanation. The Museum hired an actor to impersonate you. To make some kind of impression on the public, although why they would choose someone to impersonate *you*..." Her chin jutted forward. "This is all so strange. Although now that I'm here, I see a lot more of *me* in you. I always thought you looked more like your father. I know you took after him." She pursed her lips. "I'm not exactly awarding you with some sort of medal." She shifted her weight. "If I've become blunt in my old age, don't think me unfeeling. I love you just like I love your brother. But each of you in a different way. After all, you're two different people. I'm very proud of Apollo. He's done well for himself. He's not as smart as you in your bookish way, but he has a practical intelligence that makes him a *doer*. Anyway, like father like son. In *your* case, I mean."

"What's wrong with being like Dad? Dad put the business together. He sold it for all those millions."

She laughed.

He cocked his head. "By the time I was in high school, Dad was this icon."

She leaned back on the sofa. Her lips turned up.

Adonis perceived the image of a crocodile.

"Who *made* him an icon?" she asked. "Honestly, I've always wondered what world you live in."

Adonis shook his head.

She rolled her eyes. "Left to his own devices, your father would have spent every day doing yoga and meditating. And reading. He was always very academic. Dreamy, too. That you get from him."

"But the two of you..."

"He wasn't handsome in a classic way, your father, but he was pleasant looking enough and quite... virile."

Adonis looked down.

"You *have* discovered sex?"

Adonis let silence deliver his response—however that might be taken.

"With women, I hope. Although it's a new world, isn't it?"

"I have," he said softly. "And yes, with women."

She touched his cheek with the fingertips of her right hand. "Not that you wouldn't still be my son. On the commune, sex was rather free-form. Anyway, your father had this laid-back way about him. In college, all of us girls found it irresistible." She glanced over her shoulder as if something were creeping up behind her then turned back. "In reality, he was a very fearful man."

"But the two of you... You went to India then you lived on the commune out in the middle of nowhere."

"And he was always fearful. I blame his parents. Yes, they were your grandparents, but that doesn't change anything."

"They survived the Holocaust."

"Maybe they were strong people *then*. Or just lucky. Don't underestimate the role luck plays in people's lives. You may not remember, but your grandparents always lived in apartments. They changed addresses every year. They wanted to make it difficult for anyone to come after them."

Adonis had no memory of their moving. He was ten when his grandfather died. His grandmother died a year later. He could understand their fear, though. It may have been groundless in America, but he couldn't begin to imagine the horrors they'd experienced. "What about the store? The business Dad built?"

She closed her eyes for what seemed like half a minute then opened them. "The business that your father built?"

They were living at Daisy Dell with one-year-old Apollo. The commune was devoted to love and peace, but working the land went only so far. A meeting was called. A majority voted that everyone had to find at least a part-time job in the area. Several members left, refusing to aid and abet capitalism. Those who remained went from dissatisfied to disillusioned. "As for me, I loved the beautiful countryside, the fresh air, the quiet, but I got tired of living hand to mouth. I wasn't raised that way. Then I found out I was pregnant with you. I suppose I wanted that."

Adonis looked away.

"Well, you're here, aren't you? Anyway, I saw a for-sale sign in the window of this small grocery store in town. One of those superstores had opened just down the highway, but you wouldn't want to put anything they sold into your mouth. All those chemicals? I told your father... *told* him... *We're moving to town and buying this store. We'll get a second-hand truck and go to all the organic farms around here and hand-pick the best of what they've got and plenty of people will buy from us.* Also, there was a small apartment above the store. It was perfect."

"So Dad took it from there."

"Your father found a thousand reasons not to do it. But we did."

"But what about the money?"

"My parents agreed to lend us the money. Anything to get us out of Daisy Dell. We bought a truck and stocked up on organic produce and meat, too, beer and wine, small hardware items and hand-made crafts for tourists."

"Didn't you think you might fail?"

"I heard *failure* from your father every day for the first six months, but I put him to work behind the counter. He was good there. People liked him. We were basically outsiders, but he came off as this gentle, folksy character. With his beard and ponytail, he looked like Jerry Garcia. You know who Jerry Garcia was?"

"You guys played the Dead all the time when I was a kid."

"I did the buying from the farmers and artisans. Kept the books. Handled the advertising. We ran weekly newspaper ads and printed fliers. I put your father's picture on them. And Apollo's. People loved Apollo. Then we added you. You might not have been the cutest baby, but you use what resources you have. Everyone knew Apollo and Adonis. Still, after a while, I thought we'd made a mistake giving you boys those names. At least, from a business perspective. We should have named *you* Elijah. Your middle name. And

Apollo should have been Jacob. The Bible thumpers would have loved that."

By the time Adonis turned three, his mother noted marked differences between the two brothers. Apollo was the budding athlete and born leader. Adonis preferred playing by himself, drawing and finger painting and making things with clay. He no longer proved to be an asset. "To be honest, you were plain looking. You weren't bringing anything to the table. So, then it was just your father, me and Apollo in the ads."

Adonis raised a hand to his throat as if to release himself from a chokehold.

"Not that I didn't love you," she said. "Dropping you from the ads, that was a business decision."

Adonis studied his mother's face. He thought he saw something in her of Raphael's *Portrait of Bindo Altoviti*. A banker in Florence, Altoviti appeared almost effeminate with long blonde hair and full lips. His mother—despite the distinctly feminine nature of her hair, makeup, clothing and jewelry—struck him as somewhat androgynous. More disturbing, while Altoviti seemed to look over his right shoulder at the artist, his gaze angled a few degrees to the artist's left, the object of his attention unknowable. And what did that say about his mother's relationship with him?

She clasped her hands, appearing for a moment more the prim schoolmarm in an old western movie than the self-made businesswoman. "Adonis, you're not a child. You can handle the truth. I drove us, and your father simply got out of my way. We started making money. We expanded the store. Then a store came up for sale in another town just far enough away. And another."

After they incorporated, she made his father chairman of the board with the sole responsibility of appearing in advertising and greeting people at stores, county fairs and local festivals.

"At least you let Dad keep his beard."

"Forget those gray-haired greeters at those superstores. We had an image the superstores couldn't touch. After a while, the ponytail had to go. Times change. He wasn't happy, but I was running a company with a healthy balance sheet, and I meant to keep it that way. It was only a matter of time until some corporation made us an offer."

Adonis went to the refrigerator. "I've got bottled water. Maybe a cup of tea?"

His mother looked at her watch, its band encrusted with diamonds and emeralds.

"We could have dinner later," he said. "I could cook. Or I could take you out. I'm getting a nice raise."

"That's sweet," she said. "But the hotel limo's picking me up in five minutes. I'm going shopping then taking a nap before I meet some people for dinner." She reached into her purse, withdrew several bills and dropped them on the coffee table.

Adonis imagined it was the standard hundred dollars. He wished he could work up the nerve to refuse it. "Breakfast tomorrow?"

"I'd love to, but I have a commitment. Then I'm flying home." She stood and examined him like a rancher taking the measure of a bull before breeding her females. "It's been good talking to you, Adonis. But honestly, with all of whatever this is... I don't know who you are. Do you?"

13

Monday morning, following the distraction of handshakes and small talk, Adonis found himself seated at the conference room table to Hunter Kirk's right. He cast a self-conscious glance at Tyler Severinsen. As the next ranking Museum executive, Tyler should have occupied that seat. Not that Adonis was aware of any formal seating arrangements. He considered offering to exchange places with Tyler but feared creating an awkward moment. Besides, Tyler seemed quite content between Adonis and Mary-Louise. On the other side of the table, Lenore Josephson sat at Hunter's left flanked by Julia Edelstein, the Museum's Director of Development, and two guests.

Lenore introduced Jordan Marcus, self-professed Creative Numero Uno at Aerodrome 1, the Museum's new ad agency. Little older than Adonis, he wore jeans and an open-necked black shirt revealing the dark, curly hairs at the top of his chest. In opposition to Adonis' blue blazer and beige slacks, Jordan Marcus' clothes declared him a free spirit, a rugged individualist, an artist hell-bent on storming the barricades erected by convention.

Jordan Marcus profiled the agency's *two top honchos* who would devote a portion of their valuable time to the Museum. As for himself, he'd once been a copywriter and creative director at the city's largest agency. Despite all obstacles, he'd accumulated a walk-in closet-full of awards. *A mega-heap.* Nicole Geyer—Chief Ass Kicker—had been an account supervisor at that same hidebound agency. Pursuing *a calling to bring advertising into the twenty-second century,* they joined forces and opened their own shop. Several clients followed them. Last year they won as many major awards as the next three agencies combined. The very name of the agency attested to their approach.

"An aerodrome is an airport, right?" Jordan Marcus said.

Adonis recognized that his intonation in no way suggested a question.

"It's an old word, but the word has style," Jordan Marcus explained. "Everything we do is about style. The numeral 1? Obviously, we see ourselves as the number-one advertising agency in the city. Fuck that, in the country. Maybe not in terms of billings. Probably *never* in those terms. We're not part of some corporate behemoth. There are big accounts we wouldn't lower our standards to take on. I'm talking about being number one in creative integrity. Anything else would be number two."

Aerodrome 1 served as the departure point for world-class creative concepts and execution. *Campaigns that really take off.* But here was the thing. While the agency was consumed with being totally forward thinking, the name Aerodrome 1 evoked the pioneering, romantic days of aviation before computers sucked most of the risk out of flying. "Any good ad campaign entails a level of risk. Creative isn't worth shit unless no one's done anything like it before."

Adonis wondered how someone could use that kind of language at the Museum. And why no one batted an eye. But of course, Jordan Marcus wasn't a Museum employee. He owned a glamorous ad agency. He probably made as much money as everyone in the Department of Renaissance Art put together—Mary-Louise included.

Lenore grinned like the mother of the bride. She pointed out that Aerodrome 1 had taken on the Museum as something of a public service. They'd charge only a minimal fee.

Nicole Geyer stood.

Adonis noted Mary-Louise studying Nicole Geyer's gray silk suit. He imagined it might have cost as much as a month of his own salary. His *new* salary. She wore a silver chain around her neck, silver hoop earrings and a silver ring with what might have been a garnet on her right hand. Her left hand was bare. "We don't want you to ever be concerned that the Museum won't have our full attention," she said. "We want to give back. Jordan and I each grew up elsewhere, and we appreciate all the success we've been able to build here. In fact, we do reduced-fee work for a major anti-cancer group and work pro bono for a local women's shelter with a bare-bones budget."

"So what I want us to do," said Lenore after Nicole Geyer sat, "is get acquainted. We'll all be key players in the Museum's new ad campaign built around our upcoming Madonna and Child exhibition."

Jordan Marcus clapped his hands together. "We love the Madonna exhibit. And Jesus. Jesus is important, right? Norbertus, too. Thirty-five million, right?"

Adonis wondered if Jordan Marcus had overdosed on caffeine. Or was he playing the role of Henry the Fifth rousing the troops before the Battle of Agincourt?

The agency, Jordan Marcus continued, was placing a heavyweight team on the Museum's account. Copywriters and art directors had pledged delicate parts of their anatomies to be part of it. Moreover, they'd already started working. "Concepts. Preliminary stuff. Nothing requiring decisions now. Just to show you how we think. Totally informal. No videos, no layouts. More like storytelling."

Hunter Kirk placed his hand over his watch. "I hear what you're saying, Jordan, but isn't it a little soon?"

"Hunter, here's the thing," said Jordan Marcus. "Everyone's excited." His eyes shifted to Adonis then back to Hunter Kirk. "But this is just preliminary. To build a little momentum. Really, there's a lot more at stake than the Madonna exhibit. Every potential visitor who *doesn't* walk through your doors is lost revenue. Like an airplane that takes off with empty seats. We'll keep it short."

"Creativity is our first priority, but we also value efficiency," said Nicole Geyer. "A world-class museum is also a business." She nodded at Adonis.

Adonis smiled. Who wasn't in favor of efficiency? And while he'd have no say in the matter, he certainly was agreeable to entertaining new ideas.

TV and Internet concepts erupted from Jordan Marcus like one-liners from the stand-up comics who played the Catskill Mountains in the nineteen-fifties. "There's this contemporary Mary. Obviously, Jesus' mother but hip. She's sitting in a psychiatrist's office. Mary talks to the camera. She wonders why those Renaissance painters *never really got me*. Or we go with Baby Jesus. We superimpose a mouth on his face. He says *Okay, I raised a little hell in my time, but I was really a good guy. You can see that in my baby pictures.*" He looked around the table to gauge the attention of his audience.

"Well," said Hunter Kirk, "this is all very interesting."

"Just getting started. We see Norbertus and Cardinal Giordano in period costumes. They're strolling through the city. Hand in hand. You want to get people talking. Anyway, a crowd forms behind them. The crowd follows them as they stop for an espresso with a bunch of hipsters. The crowd keeps growing. Back on the street, this woman juggles flaming torches. Norbertus and the Cardinal join in. Then they hop a tour bus. It's filled with women in evening gowns and men in tuxedoes. The crowd runs after them. The tour bus passes a department store. We see in the windows. Mannequins are dancing. *Inside* the store windows. Finally, they run up the Museum's steps. This huge crowd is right behind them. We see this banner over the entry. It announces the Madonna and Child exhibit." He held up his right index finger. "Then the voiceover says, *You haven't seen anything until you've seen this.*"

His riff completed, Jordan Marcus sat as regal and immobile as Benvenuto Cellini's bronze of *Duke Cosimo I.* His face broke into a grin. "Okay, we're taking a little license here with Norbertus and the Cardinal. The thing is, it's all about creating buzz. Buzz is the secret sauce. Buzz *sells.*"

Adonis had no idea what to make of what he'd just heard. For that matter, he couldn't begin to guess whether anyone else at the table did, excepting Nicole Geyer.

"Okay," said Jordan Marcus. "You're thinking *Is this guy yanking our chain?* But the way it works in a creative meeting is, there's no such thing as a bad idea. You never know when something you think is crap turns out to be something you love. Alchemy. Lead into gold."

Nicole Geyer nodded.

"Last one. Close your eyes. Let this video run in your head, okay?"

Adonis closed his eyes.

"We see this bag lady."

Adonis' breath caught.

"She's scruffy but not offensive. Like your crazy grandmother. *I* had a crazy grandmother. Grandma Rose. You had to love her. At least when you weren't around her. Anyway, she's surrounded by all these bundles. Black plastic garbage bags stuffed with God knows what. You can see them, right?"

Adonis heard mumbles of assent.

"So these bags, they're full. She's digging into them like she's looking for something."

Adonis wondered where Anna was at that moment, what she was doing. Although she never appeared to be doing anything. He'd never seen her open any of her bags. He had no idea what she kept in them. Clothes, he imagined. Nothing of value. At least, to anyone but her.

"So our bag lady pulls out something here and something there. The camera cuts away to the busy street. No one notices anything. You know how it is. People absorbed in their own little worlds. We cut back to the bag lady. Whoa! She's dressed in a whole new outfit. Everything's mismatched. No worries. Her clothes, they're clean. She's done her best. She holds up a lipstick. The voiceover says *The one show everyone wants to see.*"

Throats cleared.

Adonis opened his eyes.

Jordan Marcus went on about what made a TV commercial or internet video memorable.

Adonis' thoughts turned back to Anna. He'd meant to see her, but his new life kept interfering. There were his workouts before going to the office and people wanting to go out for a drink after work. Which he did from time to time, although he drank only sparkling water. He'd also started looking for a new apartment. Finding one that wouldn't eat up his raise constituted a job in itself. Margaret the Building Manager said that a one-bedroom in his building might come vacant in a few months. The rent would be favorable, although she avoided being explicit about how *favorable* might be defined.

He sighed. He was deceiving himself if he blamed his schedule for his inattention. He'd been putting Anna off because he feared what she would think if he reappeared seemingly out of the blue. How could he explain? *We once shared something. A sense of... what? Worthlessness? Or was it something spiritual? But now, things are different. I'm Assistant Curator of Renaissance Art on a first-name basis with all the higher-ups. I'm not a failure anymore.*

Jordan Marcus paused.

Adonis abandoned his thoughts and leaned forward.

"Great creative all comes down to trust," said Jordan Marcus. "The right image. The right voice. Both. Our audience believes our message because they believe the messenger. So at the end of every TV spot or video, capping every radio commercial, in every piece of print or online ad, there's our spokesman. Yes, he's a man. Like Mary was a woman because... she was a woman. What's important is, he's someone you can't help believing. The wildest concept we can come up with? He gives it credibility. You cast this guy for any name brand. Luxury cars. Expensive watches. Whatever. Credit cards fly out of wallets. Or go the other way. Cheap light beer? Ph.Ds. in renaissance art start hauling cases of practically piss in their electric vehicles.

Hunter Kirk tilted his chair back several inches. "Are you talking about some actor, some movie star promoting the exhibition? The Museum?"

"I'm talking someone you'd feel comfortable... *privileged*... giving a briefcase filled with a million dollars in cash. *Your* cash. Your life savings. Someone you'd still love even if he ripped you off. And we unveil our guy even before the TV and videos. The Museum needs to bring more visitors in *now*, make new connections, excite people about the fall. Trust me, our guy's going to make a hell of an impression. Like the Second Coming."

"These people," said Hunter Kirk. "They get million-dollar fees."

Nancy Geyer brushed a stray hair off her forehead. "We've had some discussions at the agency. Money won't be an issue."

Adonis found himself swept up in the moment. "I think we'd all love to know who you suggest."

Jordan Marcus winked. "A few more days. We're still finalizing the concept. But I can tell you this." He held his palms together. "We're this close."

14

donis accompanied Mary-Louise and Lenore as they walked to lunch at the new French-Mediterranean restaurant tucked into an alley several blocks from the Museum. A queasy sensation nibbled at his stomach. He couldn't put his finger on what they had in mind. He tried to raise his spirits by assuring himself that they would have presented bad news in Mary-Louise's office. The attempt fell flat.

"I had to use Hunter's name to get a table," said Mary-Louise. "As far as dinner goes, forget it unless you call six weeks out."

Lenore empathized then launched a commentary on a boutique she'd recently discovered.

Adonis followed, musing that his career finally had taken off. The people at Aerodrome 1 would explain his newfound—overdue?—success in those words. While his promotion had surprised him, in no way did he consider himself undeserving. If anything, his speech at the donation ceremony along with his appearance in the media upheld the faith Mary-Louise and Tyler had placed in him. When doubts skulked about, he held them at bay by referring to the newspaper's Arts & Living section on his coffee table— his photo spread across the first page. Employing it as a prophylactic, he glanced at it each morning before leaving for work.

This morning, it left him disturbed.

As he lingered in the bathroom studying his reflection, he considered that mirrors were tools for self-deception. He could turn this way and that, tilt his head just so, adjust his posture, to some degree alter the bathroom's lighting. In this way, he could manipulate his appearance—seduce himself into seeing what he wished to see.

In contrast, his image on newsprint—flat and fixed— eliminated the mirror's illusion of dimensionality along with his sense of physical evolution, no matter how slight the changes he now experienced. The photo served as documentation stripped of delusion. Frozen in time and representing anything but a carefully composed studio portrait or publicity shot, it distanced him from self-deception. Without benefit of makeup, special lighting or a carefully determined camera angle, it revealed him not as he saw himself but as others saw him.

His image seemed perfect.

Had he become an eight-plus like Carla Parsont? A nine? He shook his head, unmindful of the people around him. Who was Adonis Licht to rank himself or anyone on a numerical scale both arbitrary and dehumanizing? Then again, he could find no rational way to dispute what he saw in the newspaper.

Adonis Licht was a ten.

As he followed Mary-Louise and Lenore around the corner, an emergency medical truck, its siren wailing, darted in and out of traffic.

Engrossed in their conversation, Mary-Louise and Lenore strode on.

Adonis halted. Across the street, he spotted Anna on one of the city's new metal benches. Unable to remember when he'd last seen her, he pondered a brief interlude before joining the women at the restaurant. Anna would be glad to see him.

That thought barely completed, he scolded himself. Did he believe that Anna required the morning lattes he brought her to get her days started? Did she care to hear his reports of mundane activities at the Museum? Had she a stake in the brief analyses he provided of his hopes and fears? If he left the city as Susan Ricketts was about to do, Anna would remain a fixture of the urban landscape along with its streetlights, traffic signs and newly installed brushed-aluminum refuse cans. He could be a ten. He could be a zero. Anna didn't need him.

But in some odd and inexplicable way, did he need Anna?

He caught up to Mary-Louise and Lenore as they entered the alley in which the restaurant was located. Rather than dark and forbidding as the alley Anna occupied, it had been cleaned up as part of a project to reclaim neglected pockets of downtown where real estate values were booming. Adonis opened the door and followed Mary-Louise and Lenore inside.

A hostess seemingly fresh out of graduate school greeted them. She wore a navy dress and pearls.

Adonis rated her minimally an eight like Carla Parsont. Here, at least, he could make some claim to objectivity. A woman had to be at least an eight to get a job in a restaurant like this.

The hostess smiled at Adonis. "You're with the Museum. That event for the Norbertus that was donated recently? You were responsible for its acquisition. I've seen the video of your speech like maybe five times. I majored in art history."

Mary-Louise and Lenore turned to Adonis.

Adonis gestured to Mary-Louise. "Actually, this lady made the acquisition. And our reservation. It's under Gelderode."

The hostess smiled. "Let me check that for you, Mr. Gelderode."

Mary-Louise glared.

The hostess glanced down at her laptop then looked up at Mary-Louise. "I'm so sorry."

As they took their seats, a silver-haired woman wearing a gray suit held her hand out to Adonis. "My husband and I attended last evening's event at the Museum," she said. "You were wonderful."

"Thank you," said Adonis. Words shaped themselves in his mouth without his summoning them. "And for supporting the Museum. Your generosity enriches life for the whole city. We couldn't conserve our rich legacy of Western art and culture without people like you."

The woman lowered her head like a parishioner receiving communion then raised it. Her smile could have illuminated one of the Museum's galleries. "I'll let you order your lunch. I know you have so much to do. And I'm going to write *another* check when I get home."

A waiter presented a wine menu.

"That," said Lenore, "is why Mary-Louise and I asked you to lunch."

Puzzled, Adonis could summon no more than a smile of his own.

"This occasion," said Mary-Louise, "calls for a glass of wine. The hell with it, a bottle." She looked at Adonis.

"Yes, that would be nice," he said, although he had no intention of drinking more than half a glass. Not if he wanted to stay fit and maintain the image he was projecting. At his workout that morning, Rob praised him effusively for rounding into what he called *near world-class shape* in only weeks. *Give credit where credit is due,* Rob said. *Your old gym? It worked for you, sure, but now you look almost like... Don't get me wrong but you're almost like one of those comic book superheroes. The kind who walked away from a nuclear bomb blast or drank some weird serum or something like that.*

They ordered a Sauvignon Blanc and decided on duck confit with spring vegetables for each. A moment later, the waiter presented a bottle to Adonis, opened it, poured a taste in Adonis' glass and awaited his approval.

Adonis nodded.

The waiter poured three glasses.

Lenore raised hers.

"I'm not sure what this is all about," Adonis said.

"We've approved the ad agency's recommendation," said Lenore. "Here's to the man who's about to give the Museum a voice... and a face."

15

The young woman who worked the gym's front desk weekday mornings stared.

Adonis lifted his right hand to his cheek and slid it down to his chin. "Did I miss a spot?"

"No, your shave looks really close. I was just thinking that one of those three-day growths would look great on you. Most young guys with a growth think they look sexy and dangerous, but they just look like posers. Old guys look like pervs."

He rested a hand above his hair.

"You probably get out of bed, and your hair just puts itself together. I'd like to see *that*." She raised a hand to her mouth.

Adonis smiled to communicate that no, she hadn't made a suggestive remark—at least not one that offended him.

"Anyway," she said, "Rob's here."

Adonis changed and went to the weight room. Two men and a woman who'd arrived even earlier worked the machines.

The door opened and closed behind him.

"Looks like somebody's serious about his workout this morning," Rob said.

"It gets light so early this time of year."

Rob drew closer. "If you don't mind, I had a thought. Something you might find interesting."

"Sure," said Adonis.

Rob watched Adonis go through his usual warmup of pushups, light stretching and rotations. Then he led Adonis to the bench press station. The gym offered all the latest machines with their complicated gears and pulleys, and digitized measurements, but Rob considered free weights superior. *You're not just lifting with your arms or legs. With free weights your entire body works to maintain balance. Much better for your core.*

The bar held small weighted discs at either end. "So I was thinking," Rob said. He looked around the room.

The other members remained intent on their workouts.

Rob turned back to Adonis. "Don't take this the wrong way, but you're not exactly the average guy who comes in here. Not that we don't get athletes. You've seen them. Only you're kind of..."

"An anomaly?" Adonis asked.

Rob grinned. He looked relieved. "Anyway, I was thinking... wondering... how many reps you could do benching two twenty-five. You being an anomaly."

"What's special about two-twenty-five?"

"That's the weight pro football scouts use at their predraft combine to strength-test linemen coming out of college. The thing is, those guys are way bigger than you. You're more like a wide receiver or a safety. The linemen, they're beasts. They weigh two-eighty, three hundred, threetwenty, more. Sometimes way more. Really, I think it would be interesting."

Despite the physical changes he'd undergone, Adonis didn't feel particularly competitive. Not like Apollo, who would have required no encouragement. Still, Rob's suggestion intrigued him. "How many reps do these guys do?"

"I'd rather not say until you give it a try. If you want to."

Adonis lay back on the bench, placed his feet flat on the floor and positioned his head beneath the bar.

"The weight on there now," said Rob. "You can warm up with that."

Adonis bent his arms at his elbows and stretched. Then he gripped the bar.

Rob helped him remove the bar from the rack and stood behind his head to spot him.

Adonis raised and lowered the bar ten times.

Rob helped place the bar back in the rack. "How do you feel?"

Adonis slipped out from under the bar and stood. "Good. Really. I feel good."

Rob set the weights. "Two twenty-five." He screwed up his face. His eyes almost disappeared. "Okay, so a word of caution. It's not like you can't bench two twenty-five. No big deal there. The thing is, it's not the weight by itself. It's the reps. Only you don't want to push yourself to the point where you tear something. You're not getting drafted, right?"

Adonis slid back under the bar.

"Take it slow," said Rob. Again, he helped un-rack the bar.

The muscles in Adonis' arms, chest and shoulders raised and lowered the bar upward with machine-like regularity. Short of exhaustion but heeding Rob's advice, he settled the bar into the rack.

"Jesus!" said Rob. His voice echoed Jordan Marcus' excitement. "Twenty-seven! The strongest college linemen generally go mid-to upper-thirties. I'm talking about just the *top* guys. With a little more work, you might match them. And you being you, I'm thinking you won't have to bulk up." He patted Adonis on the shoulder. "No offense, but this is kind of freaky."

16

donis tightened his grip on the large manila envelope under his arm. "I'm really sorry," he told the hostess. "I should have made a reservation. I know how busy lunch gets." A mea culpa, he reasoned, might encourage her to look kindly on him. He turned to Carla Parsont. "Honestly, with all the work... It just slipped my mind."

The hostess smiled. "Welcome back. Norbertus of Hannover, right?"

"Norbertus is the painter. Was. I'm not him."

"Yes, of course. I mean, no. I mean, you're the Museum Man."

"Museum Man," said Carla Parsont. "Very catchy."

"And you're here with another beautiful woman," the hostess said. She held a hand up to her mouth.

Adonis again turned to Carla. "Mary-Louise and Lenore. A business lunch."

"*This,*" said Carla, "is a business lunch."

Adonis felt a tinge of disappointment. He understood that it was a business lunch, but he hoped it might become something more.

The hostess surveyed the restaurant. "You really caught us at a busy time, Mr. Licht."

Adonis' eyes widened.

She smiled. "I'll have a table in five minutes."

Adonis caught Carla looking at him with what he took as admiration.

"Would you like wine?" he asked after they were seated.

"I'd love a glass," she said. "Two glasses wouldn't hurt. But no. We're not supposed to drink when we're working. Corporate policy. I'm not quite senior enough to break it, and believe me, all the senior people do. Back in the day, reporters drank all the time. *Way* back in the day they got most of their news in bars. The old version of websites kids in Macedonia or places like that create to post fake news. We have people at the paper who do nothing but monitor that stuff. Anyway, my alcohol tolerance isn't all that great."

"Mine neither," said Adonis. He took the manila envelope off his lap and placed it on the table.

A waiter came for their drink orders.

"Water's fine for both of us," Adonis said.

They scanned the menu.

A busboy set down a basket of rolls.

Adonis held the basket out to Carla.

"No thanks," she said. "Cutting down on carbs."

"I don't think that seems to be a problem."

"Coming from you, that's a compliment."

"I try to be careful about what I eat."

"You'd think. Are you also a triathlete or something like that?"

"I work out, that's all."

"Me, too, but it's obvious *your* workouts are way past *mine* or any of the guys' at my gym. And you still have your clothes on."

"You could get a better look," Adonis said. He rocked back in his seat, both fearing he'd overstepped his bounds and wondering when he'd developed the nerve.

Carla's eyes sparkled. A faint upturn registered at the corners of her mouth. "So you mentioned you have information I can use. Does it have anything to do with Mary-Louise Gelderode?"

"Everything about the Madonna and Child exhibition has something to do with Mary-Louise."

"I'm sure. I was just wondering if Lenore asked you to set me up." She flipped her hair. "I don't mean that in a negative way. Manipulating me or anything like that. Besides, never happen."

"No. Of course not."

"It's just that I've been assigned to do a profile on her. Mary-Louise. She's got quite a reputation." She grinned. "I mean, as a player at the Museum. What I'm doing now is talking to people, gathering background. My editor thinks the profile should come out this fall just before the Madonna and Child exhibit opens."

"Exhibition. It's called an exhibition."

"Right. Yes. Anyway, this fall. Maximum exposure. Lenore agrees."

Adonis tapped his index finger on the envelope. "What's here is some new information about Norbertus."

"You could have emailed me."

"Then we wouldn't be having lunch. Also, with email there are always security issues."

"You're not telling me the President of the United States loves Norbertus, so he's coming to the opening, are you?"

Adonis shook his head.

"So anyway, I'm thinking you've got something new on Norbertus."

The waiter returned. They ordered salads.

Carla took her digital recorder out of her purse.

Adonis slid the envelope towards her.

She withdrew a manuscript of a dozen pages.

"It's an academic paper," he said. "It's going to be delivered tomorrow afternoon at a conference in Zurich by Antonio Camilleri. Dr. Camilleri's a professor of art history at Sapienza University of Rome. Mary-Louise met him at Oxford. They keep in touch."

Carla glanced at the title page.

"I've highlighted the most relevant information. I've also arranged for you to talk to Dr. Camilleri after lunch. It's evening there. He's expecting your call."

Carla scanned the paper, noting the highlights Adonis had marked in yellow. "Interesting."

Fred filled the doorway to Adonis' office. "Long lunch out, and you're still working?"

"We all work, right?"

"Some more than others." Fred looked around the office. "Still a damn impressive sight."

Adonis held his arms out. "It looked bigger when Sue Ricketts worked here. It's barely bigger than a closet. A walk-in closet, anyway."

"Don't bitch to *me*. I'm still waiting to see if I have to share space with some kid fresh out of grad school. Or maybe they won't fill your old position, which means me and everyone else in the department will be busting our balls."

"I assume you mean that figuratively," said Adonis. He nodded at the chair in front of his desk.

Fred sat, angling his legs to provide space for his knees. "So anyway, boss, things are getting interesting."

"I'm not your boss."

"The hell you're not."

"Not like you make it sound. And what's so interesting about me having an office?"

"I'm not talking about your office. I'm talking about your friend and the article she wrote. And I hope you've got something going there, because if you don't, I'll be glad to give it a shot."

"Carla Parsont? Her article about Dr. Camilleri's paper?"

"Yes, her and that, and I'm pissed."

"Pissed? Hunter, Tyler and Mary-Louise all love it."

"Sure, they love it," said Fred. "Scandal sells." He pointed at Adonis. "But you left me out of the loop. I had to read the article online this morning to find out what the hell it was all about. Which makes you an insider and me an outsider."

"Dr. Gelderode and Lenore Jacobson didn't want me to release any of the details to the department staff."

Fred's eyes rolled up. "You have an office. You have secrets. And now I notice we're back to referring to *Dr. Gelderode*. Like I've been saying, it's all about the overlords and the underlings."

Adonis held his palms out to signify that he didn't want an argument, nothing had changed, they'd still enjoy the same camaraderie even if some things *had* changed. His attention shifted from Fred's look of skepticism to his hands. They struck him as the hands of an athlete. That morning at the gym, a group of men asked him to play basketball. He'd never liked basketball, yet he agreed. While not much of a shooter, he outran and out-jumped everyone. Someone asked if he'd played in college and might want to play in a league the gym ran. People spoke that way to Apollo.

Fred stuck his chin out. "Admit it. You got caught with your pants down."

Adonis transferred his gaze back to Fred. "You're right. Her name is Mary-Louise. I should refer to her as Mary-Louise. Between you and me anyway. This is all kind of new."

Fred scratched the top of his head. "So Camilleri dug up some dirt. So more people are going to come to the Madonna and Child exhibition so they can see what Norbertus of Hannover is all about. Works for me. It helps us keep our jobs." He tapped his knuckles together. "But what if some noses on the faces of some of the big-money people who support the Museum get bent out of shape? What then?"

"You think the scholarship's questionable?"

"It's not the scholarship."

"Because I have a copy of Camilleri's paper for you. It's pretty much straightforward. Norbertus wrote three letters to Cardinal Giordano. Camilleri had them analyzed. Paper. Ink. Norbertus' signature. All good."

Adonis' cell beeped. He gestured toward the door. "I have a radio interview. And a TV crew is coming by."

Fred stood. "Fine. You're in the public eye. I get that. What I *don't* get is how Norbertus would have been dumb enough to put all that stuff down on paper."

17

A series of light taps interrupted Adonis the following morning as he scanned an email from his counterpart working for Randolph Bennett. He looked up to find Mary-Louise standing in the doorway.

"You don't have to knock," Adonis said. "Not *you*."

Mary-Louise brushed a finger along the corner of her right eye. "Yes, I do. You're a senior member of the team now."

Adonis started to motion her forward then lowered his hand. He stood.

Mary-Louise remained in the doorway.

Adonis sat.

"I'm sorry," she said. Her voice betrayed a slight quaver.

Noticing that her eyes were red-rimmed, he found himself at a loss for words. He'd seldom seen women cry—certainly not his mother. Not even at his father's funeral. And now Mary-Louise of all people. He opened the upper desk drawer at his left and held up a box of tissues. "Susan left these."

She held out her hand.

Adonis wanted to leap over the desk, place his arm around her shoulders and hold her close. And who knew? The way she'd been acting around him lately, the way she looked at him now, maybe that was what she wanted him to do. But Mary-Louise Gelderode and Adonis Licht? He remained seated.

Mary-Louise dabbed at her eyes then blew her nose.

Adonis reached below the desk and held his small metal wastebasket aloft.

She pulled out his lone visitor chair.

Uncomfortable with her silence, he asked, "Anything wrong?"

She sat, stood, closed the door then sat again.

Adonis considered words of consolation. *It'll be fine. Everything's going to work out. Tomorrow's another day. There's even still this afternoon.* But what would he be consoling her about? He offered a smile of encouragement the way therapists did in films.

Mary-Louise's face blended agitation with sorrow.

Adonis held to his silence. The more upset she seemed, the more a sense of calm—even self-satisfaction—flooded over him.

She slumped in her chair as if she'd aged forty or fifty years since entering his office. "I just had two phone calls."

Adonis nodded. Movie therapists always nodded to encourage their patients to continue.

Her white, even teeth pressed down on her lower lip.

Adonis waited then repeated back what she'd told him. "You just had two phone calls."

"One was personal," she said. She shook her head. "I really shouldn't be telling you this."

"You don't have to," he said. He could think of no more perfect way to encourage her to do just that, to engage in a level of intimacy with him that once would have represented nothing other than a fantasy.

"No, I don't," she said. "I know that."

Adonis nudged a small stack of folders.

"Still, they were very upsetting. Unexpected."

He rested his chin on his right fist.

She sniffled. "We all have our disappointments, don't we?" She straightened. Her jaw jutted out in a display of courage and determination. "We move on."

He nodded.

Her jaw reset itself. "The other call was from Randolph Bennett. He said his people have been sending you little odds and ends... his words... concerning Norbertus. Also, stray thoughts on the rest of the exhibition."

Adonis gestured towards his laptop.

"Anything I should know about?"

They'd gone back to business, but he could hide his disappointment. What right had he to pry into her thoughts? "We're ready to move on with the exhibition panels, the brochure, the catalog... that's obviously a big job... and the educational materials. The audio tour, of course. We'll sell a lot of audio tours."

"Randolph is quite pleased. He's a wonderful colleague but a bit anal."

Adonis' stomach fluttered. Was Mary-Louise setting him up, testing whether he'd criticize Randolph, an old and valued colleague? If so, to what purpose? She was the one who proposed his promotion to Tyler and Hunter. "So there's no problem with Randolph then," he said.

"Not at all. It's just that he asked a favor."

"What sort of favor?"

"Randolph's been getting an earful from Cardinal O'Hare about the article on Norbertus and Cardinal Giordano. The story by what's-her-name."

"Carla. Parsont."

"Not that Randolph, who's a former Catholic by the way, can't handle it. He and O'Hare are friends." Her face contorted. "Very close friends."

"Randolph and...?"

"I'm not implying anything, but Randolph's never been the type to pretend to be anything other than what he is."

Adonis sat sculpture-still. He saw no point in revealing that Randolph had come on to him when they'd first met.

"Anyway, Randolph thought he'd throw Cardinal O'Hare a bone. Smooth ruffled feathers by showing him the painting. Let him see what a wonderful piece of art it is."

"So he's flying here with Cardinal O'Hare?"

"No. He wants us to ship the painting to him. I think he also wants to give his staff a little jolt since obviously we're hosting the exhibition first, taking advantage of the Christmas season and all that. Randolph wants his people to maintain their excitement."

"Fred can call our shipper."

"I'll feel better, Adonis, if you give it your personal attention. So will Randolph."

"Yes, of course. But isn't this a little unusual? And when do we get the painting back?"

"Three weeks. And yes, moving a masterpiece around is the last thing we want to do, but we do it all the time. Art pieces are coming in from all over the world for this exhibition. What's important here is, the Museum owes Randolph. He lent us that Rembrandt a few years ago and never made a fuss. Also, he'll cover the shipping and insurance costs from his budget."

"No problem. I'll take care of it."

Mary-Louise's chin dropped to her chest. Motionless, she sat head down like a mathematician calculating a challenging equation. She took a deep breath. Her breasts rose then gently fell. When she looked up, the sparkle had returned to her eyes. "You've become a major asset to this department," she said. "More so to the Museum, given your added responsibilities as the Museum's spokesperson."

"I appreciate the opportunity. I really do."

"I'm sure, but I hope you fully appreciate all that your new role involves. There are so many fine lines to walk. Of course, Lenore's covered a lot of that ground with you, but as your manager, I think the two of us should take things a step further. Nothing formal. A casual conversation. Away from the Museum would be best. Just so we can be clear about what we expect from you and, well, what you need from us."

"Alright," he said.

"Then that's settled. Dinner. Saturday night."

18

Red and blue lights on two patrol cars momentarily flashed in unison with the red and yellow lights on an emergency services truck. Nothing out of the ordinary for a Saturday night in the city—even at this early an hour. As the lights shifted back to their disparate rhythms, Adonis joined several well-dressed onlookers held back by a uniformed policeman. On the sidewalk, a few feet beyond the officer, a yellow plastic sheet covered what appeared to be a human body. Heart pounding, he uttered a mute "Anna."

A man Adonis' age wearing lightly faded jeans and a navy blazer resembling his appeared at his side. "Can't really tell much," said the man. "Although that looks like the toe of a man's shoe peeking out." He stepped away as if he'd peered into a bakery window but decided to pass.

Adonis struggled to retain his composure. The shape beneath the plastic sheet *did* appear to be longer and thinner than Anna's might be no matter how grotesquely distorted by death. Concealed in however many layers of clothing she wore even on a warm evening like this, her shape would have taken a noticeably different form. *Plumper* seemed a kind word. But he'd hardly been foolish to fear that Anna had left this world on that strip of concrete. How could living on the streets not put her or anyone at risk? It occurred to him that he'd uncovered the reason he hadn't seen Anna—had, in truth, been avoiding her. He'd always known on some level that he might lose her at any time. The sudden insight sparked a sense of urgency. He'd have to look for her as soon as he found the time,

Adonis stepped back and reproached himself. What purpose did it serve to indulge in morbid speculation? Anna had kept herself safe for years. Besides, she would have been totally out of place—out of character—sheltering in an upscale neighborhood with its tree-lined streets, expensive residential buildings, restaurants, cafes and boutiques. And with a matching police presence to protect those with considerable stakes in the area. Hardly Anna's habitat.

He bit his knuckles in an act of contrition. *Habitat?*

Adonis walked on. The condominium and apartment buildings grew more impressive, the shops more elegant, the quiet more noticeable.

He stopped at a high-rise with expansive glass windows tinted light blue. An arched glass canopy sheltered the entryway. Brushed aluminum numerals designated the street address. The font seemed suited to the design scheme of a contemporary arts museum. No doubt the building offered every amenity someone with money and taste could desire. He extended his hand towards the intercom and dialed.

"Adonis?" asked Mary-Louise.

As the elevator rose to the tenth floor just below the top of the building, Adonis considered that Mary-Louise's invitation might be a ruse, that she intended to disarm him before presenting unanticipated bad news. Dismissing the urge to go back down and call from the street with an excuse—a nervous reaction understandable but unbecoming—he found her apartment. After taking his coat, Mary-Louise lowered herself next to Adonis on the long sofa covered in dove-gray leather and accented with pillows in manganese violet and turquoise. Black slacks—Adonis had only seen her in skirts and dresses—made her legs appear even longer while deemphasizing the slight turn-in of her left foot. A sleeveless top of shimmering silver emphasized the age-defying uplift of her breasts. Who paid attention to feet, Adonis thought, given breasts like that? Her dark hair hung loose over her shoulders. She poured two glasses of white wine.

Adonis raised his glass to his nose. It seemed like the right thing to do.

She raised her own and touched it to his. "Tchin-tchin."

Adonis sipped. He hadn't been drinking much wine lately, although he'd noticed that after those rare occasions when he'd had a full glass or even a second and even overeaten by his now exacting standards, his weight remained unaffected.

Mary-Louise lowered her glass. "Hungry? I'm ravenous."

"Can I help with dinner?" Adonis asked. It seemed the proper thing to say, although sitting with Mary-Louise in her living room, her figure so prominently displayed, stripped the prospect of dinner of whatever importance it might have had. He urged himself to focus. Officially, Mary-Louise had invited him to her condo to discuss his growing responsibilities at the Museum and the challenges they would pose. Undoubtedly, she had a clearer concept than he of all that was involved and the direction his career was taking. It was one thing to fantasize about promotions with their accompanying pay raises and relationships with successful people, another to make sense of his unexpectedly rapid ascent—to decode what he'd become and anticipate where that might lead. Still, meeting in Dr. Mary-Louise Gelderode's condo on a Saturday night to discuss Museum business? Was that what he was doing here? "I can cut vegetables," he said. "Things like that."

She threw her head back and laughed. "I'm not much of a cook. Of course, looking at my kitchen you'd think otherwise. I had dinner delivered from one of my favorite restaurants. They do a fabulous salmon. It heats up beautifully in the steam oven."

Adonis sought to respond with a clever remark but couldn't come up with anything. Which was odd. At least, now. Not long ago, he'd stood before the Museum's guests to welcome the donation of Clark Merrill's Norbertus, and for the first time in his life, words had come effortlessly. At meetings and lunches that followed, his most offhand comments received accolades. Often, he didn't even have to open his mouth to be credited with uncommon wisdom. Now, as Mary-Louise's eyes fixed on his, his thoughts stumbled over each other like panicked rats fleeing a burning building. His eyes found a high-quality print of Leonardo's *Lady with an Ermine* then wandered to a modern piece.

"The Miró's a copy but a damn good one," she said. "My ex and I found it in Paris. It came with the settlement." She shifted her weight towards him.

Adonis' skin tingled. "I didn't know you were married. *Had* been married."

"I didn't know the fucker was an abusive bastard until our wedding night. We crashed and burned years ago. My lawyers stuck it to him. He paid for the condo. Well, the condo before this one. I sold it. I paid the difference for this one in cash. *His* cash."

"I'm sorry," Adonis said.

She placed a hand on his knee then removed it. "I shouldn't have used that language." She raised her wine glass. "This isn't my first glass, either, but fuck it. Anyway, after I found out he was fucking around on me, *I* started

fucking around. With, among other people, the same man."
She placed her free hand on his. "Adonis, you have no idea
how quickly you can get a divorce when your husband
doesn't give a shit about you or how much it costs. I suppose
it's like everything else in life. It's all about how much you
want something."

Adonis looked slightly away to demonstrate that he had
no desire to peek behind the curtain concealing whatever
dark secrets Mary-Louise had accumulated.

She shifted again and poured another glass of wine. "This
may be my third. Could be my fourth. Actually, I may be a
little drunk. Well, not drunk. Buzzed. Just a little. Maybe
more than a little." She raised a finger and wagged it. "But
not shitfaced."

Adonis nodded the way people did when they had no
choice but to acknowledge an embarrassing truth without
calling undue attention to that truth or its teller.

"Don't worry about dinner," she said. "It'll only take ten
minutes." A soft sigh escaped between her cadmium-red
lips.

"Maybe this wasn't a good idea," he said.

"No, no. It's just... All this wine before dinner. Very
unprofessional. If I pride myself on anything, it's my fucking
professionalism." She took his hand. "Honestly, Adonis, I
didn't ask you to dinner to tell you my problems." She leaned
closer and closed her eyes.

He watched her lips approach. The scent of her perfume—
her entire being—entered him like a wraith whose passion he
lacked the power to resist despite the danger it evoked. Her
tongue caressed his. It tasted less of desire than desperation.

Light from the building across the street gave muted definition to the edges of the draperies covering the bedroom's large windows. From there Adonis' eyes darted over the room's diverse contours made discernable by a small night light at floor level. They found the outlines of a chair, vanity, dresser and slim armoire resembling his mother's jewelry chest. Drawing closer, they rested on Mary-Louise, asleep on her side.

Despite the darkness, the bedroom's features offered more clarity than did his sense of time. He had no idea how long they'd made love. *Had sex*, he corrected himself. He'd never understood exactly what *making love* entailed. Probably because he'd never been in love. *Fucked*, Fred would have presented it bluntly. Not that Fred would ever find out what had just happened—unless he somehow intuited it, which was not impossible. Adonis conjectured that Fred possessed some sort of sixth sense, a quality almost as bizarre as his own inexplicable transformation. For that matter, he suspected that everyone possessed some curious quality that defied logic. And what did that mean? Had he come to terms with his new self? He would be ungrateful to complain—to what or whom remained the mystery—but he had yet to develop a reasonable definition of his new self. Did it represent only the physical change he'd experienced? Or had he also undergone some internal mutation as real but far more subtle? He wondered whether he'd failed to recognize a loosening of his moorings, a slow drifting away from himself.

Mary-Louise shifted beneath the sheet. A strand of her hair snaked against his cheek.

Adonis' thoughts wandered to Botticelli's *Venus and Mars*. Venus, fully awake and in the company of youthful satyrs, gazes at the near-naked and semi-comatose Mars, exhausted by his sexual encounter with the goddess of love and desire. A reversal of roles, he supposed, was only fair.

What, he wondered, had happened? He understood that they'd made love, had sex, fucked. He appreciated that he'd never experienced anything like it. Acknowledging the limits of his experience, he'd never been in bed with a woman who'd responded to him as Mary-Louise had. What might have passed for a smile abandoned his lips, yielding to a sense of shame. He could just as well have performed in a porn flick, gone through the motions with striking proficiency solely for the pleasure of men for whom he served as an alter ego, sating a desire they would never themselves quench.

Or was something more involved? The matter defied any simple explanation. Here he lay beside this insanely beautiful woman—a symbol of erotic perfection despite her foot—who like him, represented less the product of human evolution than a constructed work animated by an unknown force. Without cessation, she'd filled the bedroom with gasps and moans. Uttered cries of *Oh my god*. Screamed his name. Implored him to *Fuck me oh yes just like that just like that don't stop oh god don't stop*. During both her orgasms, she bellowed *I'm coming I'm coming I'm coming I'm coming* with an intensity marathon in length and seemingly beyond endurance. After, she gasped for breath then asked, *Did you come? Did you? Was it good?*

Her question triggered the memory of a joke told by old Jewish comedians. *Sex? I'll tell you about sex. When it's good, it's great. And when it's bad? It's still good.*

Adonis looked away when he replied, *Yes.*

He could not evade the thought that what someone like Fred might consider an unparalleled sexual conquest unnerved him. Did sex represent Mary-Louise's only interest in him? His only interest in her? That might be enough for most men, but was it sufficient for him? Even if Fred would mock him for admitting it—not that he would ever disclose what had just happened—the experience had lacked something essential. He'd felt no emotional closeness. Whether that disparaged him as less than manly, he *wanted* that closeness. And what did Mary-Louise want? She may have been needy, but that wasn't the same thing. And where would her neediness end? He wondered if she might seek— no, not seek, *demand*—more Saturday nights from him. Make sex the price of his promotion. Fred would pay it in a heartbeat. Adonis had misgivings. That kind of relationship posed a substantial measure of risk. At some point, Mary-Louise could—inevitably *would*—lose interest in him. Then what? Would she throw him under the bus?

Misgivings rampaged through his head then faded as Adonis found himself suspended in that all-too-familiar yet disturbing intersection between wakefulness and sleep. Confined in a state as surreal and frightening as William Blake's watercolor of *Job's Evil Dreams*, he remained as powerless to extricate himself as a rabbit snared in a wire noose. Although there was no ledge outside Mary-Louise's window, he heard pigeons emitting raucous coos aping the shifting of gears in a giant earthmover. He pressed his hands against his ears—or thought he did—while watching himself spread his arms like wings and leap down the three flights of stairs from his apartment. The stairs gave way. Nothing solid met the soles of his bare feet. He reached for the handle of the lobby door. It swung open, detached from its hinges and floated off in a river of air glowing in the darkness as if composed of all the world's fireflies. Mary-Louise in a white ball gown appeared standing on a deserted sidewalk. Pigeon shit encased her feet up to her ankles. Behind her, a street lamp hovered like an elongated black hummingbird. Its bulb blinked Morse code—*dot-dot-dot, dash-dash-dash, dot-dot-dot.* Adonis found himself in her place. The pigeon shit rose to his shins then to his knees. He attempted to cry for help. His lips and tongue formed the words *Cinderella! Cinderella!* No sound left his throat. A burst of light flared. Anna appeared sitting on a giant black plastic bag suspended in air like a flying carpet. She wore a gown identical to Mary-Louise's. A folded black plastic bag entwined her from her right shoulder to her left hip like the sash on a beauty queen. He probed her face but could discern only her eyes shining like flames flickering atop candles. *What is this?* he attempted to call out. The words lurched from his throat, emerging as hoarse groans. Anna began to chant. Her tone replicated the sweet and comforting nature of his mother's voice when she sang to him as a child because she still loved him not for what he might become but for who he was. *All that glitters,* Anna crooned. *All that glitters.*

19

Two blocks from the Museum on an otherwise ordinary Tuesday morning, Adonis suspected that someone was following him. Seeing no advantage in betraying his uneasiness, he maintained his pace. Besides, what could he possibly be alarmed about? The streets teemed with people on their way to work. Added to that, according to Rob, he was something of a freak. He could take care of himself.

The light at the corner turned red. The familiar orange hand, a proxy mother of sorts, admonished him not to enter the crosswalk. He waited as vehicles accelerated and jockeyed for position like mechanical whitewater raging through a canyon of brick, concrete, glass and steel.

Someone tapped his shoulder.

He turned.

A woman smiled.

Blonde with sunglasses perched atop a slender nose and a wide mouth highlighted by lipstick in Chinese vermilion, she projected the ephemeral attractiveness of a youngish matron just starting to put on weight but determined to wage an unremitting if unwinnable battle against time and gravity.

She placed a still-delicate hand on his forearm. "I hope you don't mind, but I saw you when I got off the bus," she said. "I feel so foolish, but I know I've seen you before."

"I'm sorry," said Adonis. "I don't think so." Choosing tact over annoyance, he added, "If I'd seen *you*, I'd have remembered."

"Oh, that's so sweet. But of course, you wouldn't have seen *me*. I'm no one. *You're* the *Museum Man*."

Adonis stood motionless and silent.

"Your photo?" said the woman. Her lilting voice eroded the boundary between statement and question. "It's on all the buses. And that ad in yesterday's arts section. The newspaper?"

Adonis nodded. The woman had reminded him that over the past weeks since he'd slept with Mary-Louise, ads created by Aerodrome 1 and featuring the Museum Man had popped up on buses, taxis and billboards of all sizes. Still, he often found a disconnect between the man who encouraged people to visit the Museum and himself.

"You don't have to admit it, but you don't really work for the Museum," she confided, her voice near hushed despite the urban symphony of roaring engines, squealing tires and honking horns. "You're an actor."

Adonis considered that in some ways, he was.

"I've seen you in the movies, right? Or on TV. Probably both." She placed her free hand over her heart. "Give me a minute."

The light turned green. A small crowd lingered at the curb, blocking Adonis' path.

A young woman wearing jeans and a lavender sleeveless blouse approached. She rummaged through a canvas bag large enough to carry her belongings on a short beach vacation and retrieved an envelope and a pen. "Can I have your autograph?" she asked.

Not wanting to disappoint her and risk provoking a small disturbance, Adonis signed the envelope.

Another woman held up a magazine.

The young matron tightened her grip. "Now I know. You were on that TV series about the detective who killed his wife. Or no, you were the surgeon..."

An attractive young woman in a cream-colored suit handed Adonis a business card and mouthed two words.

Adonis read her lips: *Call me.*

Fred's head floated inside the doorframe of Adonis' office. "Mary-Louise just got in maybe ten minutes ago. She must think I'm her admin or assistant admin or whatever, because she told me she wants to see you. ASAP."

Adonis checked his cell. It was eleven-fifteen.

"When you're the department Curator in Charge, you can come in late whenever you want, right? That or if you're the Museum Man you can do whatever you want." He disappeared like the assistant in a magician's vanishing act.

Adonis found Mary-Louise behind her desk, her hands clasped on its surface.

"Close the door, please," she said.

Adonis closed the door and sat.

"Before I came in today," she went on, "I stood by that large photo of you near the main entrance. I don't know how long. People stopped and not just women. Men, too. I saw them."

Embarrassed, Adonis replied, "Paying visitors, I hope."

Mary-Louise brushed the side of her hair with her fingertips. "So I came in late, but don't think I was shirking my responsibilities. I mentor a girl in middle school. Trisha. Seventh grade. All the mentors in her class were asked to come to a special assembly. I won't bore you with the details, but I assure you, there's nothing boring about mentoring a twelve-year-old girl."

Adonis couldn't imagine Mary-Louise mentoring a child. She'd certainly never mentioned it.

"What I want to tell you is, I didn't want to come in today. Here. To work. I didn't have to. There's nothing you can't handle. At least for a day or so." Her face paled. "I've been thinking, Adonis. I've been confused, and I want to get this right." Her voice dropped to a whisper. "What happened between us last month... It can't happen again."

Adonis took a breath.

"We've been tiptoeing around it, keeping each other at arm's length despite the normal work routine because we both know it was a foolish mistake."

Unsure of the response she expected—if, indeed, she expected one—Adonis scratched the back of his neck.

"Not that that night together wasn't thrilling, you understand." She bit her lips. "But unprofessional."

Adonis dropped his chin to his chest like an eight-year-old caught outside a grocery store, his pockets stuffed with contraband candy. Perhaps he *was* an actor. Whatever had come up for Mary-Louise, *he* felt no remorse. Awkwardness, yes. Tons of that. Remorse? *He* hadn't seduced *her*. She could have thought about what was and wasn't professional before she invited him to her condo—before they went to bed together. Still, he was in no position to call her on the matter.

"What I'm saying, Adonis, is that I never intended for that to happen." She turned away. "Which, of course, is a lie. A ridiculous lie. It was exactly what I planned. What I *knew* would happen. Well, *hoped*. It's just that I... I received some bad news a few days earlier. A personal matter. I think I alluded to that once. It was unsettling. Well, that's a lie, too. It was *upsetting*. I have emotions like anyone else. It's just that given my position..." She turned back to him. "Each of us at the Museum has a responsibility to act in the most professional manner. I simply needed to feel like a woman. An *attractive* woman. You can understand that, can't you?"

Adonis hesitated. She'd thrust him into totally new territory. Of course, he understood that every woman wanted to feel attractive. Beautiful. But Mary-Louise *was* beautiful. Perhaps, for no explicable reason, she didn't see herself the way others saw her. As for him, all he knew about her was what he saw on the surface. A certain arrangement of skin, bones and muscle. Hair, eyes and lips. Beyond the way she addressed her professional duties, what went on *inside* her remained concealed. Like her mentoring a child. And the bad news she'd mentioned. Had something happened to some member of her family? He had no inkling as to what family she had. Did a friend have a problem? He knew nothing of her friends. Had she been turned down for a position at another museum—a more prestigious position with a bigger salary? Surely, her present position was impressive enough. Or was the concept of *enough* a myth?

Adonis wondered if a man might be involved. Obviously not Adonis Licht. But he knew nothing about what men she saw. For that matter, he had no idea whether she saw men at all. He wondered if, despite—or evidenced by—her awkward marriage and their one-night stand, she was a lesbian long suffocating in the closet. Unless she liked men *and* women. He didn't think of himself as all that naïve, but she occupied a space outside the limits of his comprehension. Not that he could tell her that she confused him. She'd probably collapse into tears. Disintegrate. He accepted the lone alternative he saw available. "I understand."

Color returned to Mary-Louise's cheeks. "Well then, we agree that we've been there and done that, and that's the end of it."

"It was good while it lasted, though," he said then instantly reproached himself. Their relationship—he didn't know what else to call it—had consisted of a single night. Nonetheless, he felt some vague obligation to leave her office having lifted her spirits. It was the least he could do.

"One more thing," she said. "Our Norbertus is coming back tomorrow. Obviously, it's a bit later than we anticipated, but Randolph wanted a little extra time. What's more, he's flying back with it. He wants to meet with us."

"I'll go to the airport."

She waved her hand. "Randolph is coming in with one of his staff."

"Is there anything I should know?"

She sighed. "If I had to guess, Randolph has ferreted out some important new information on Norbertus. Something the media will fall all over. Something that will probably land you on TV again before the ad agency shoots our TV and internet commercials. Something for which he can take credit." Having emerged from the depths of her sorrow, she now seemed on the verge of laughter. "Or maybe he just wanted another excuse to come visit us and someone he met, I'm told, at the donation gala. All on his expense account, of course." She smiled. "Honestly, what more could he have come up with?"

20

nna accepted her morning latté and muffin with gloved hands then lowered the white paper bag containing the muffin to the alley's asphalt bed. Looking up, her eyes registered neither surprise nor reprimand.

"I'm sorry," he said, holding his cup of plain coffee. "I know it's been a long time. A month maybe? Longer?" He searched for a hint of disapproval.

Her eyes expressed only the willingness to listen.

"So anyway, we're going to shoot some TV commercials for the Museum. That and some videos for the internet and social media. I'll be telling people all about Norbertus of Hannover and the big exhibition coming up. I'm supposed to see the scripts soon. It should go okay. It's not like it used to be. I don't have any problem speaking to people during meetings or in presentations. The words just come. People respond like I'm saying something really important." He glanced at his coffee, untouched since he left the café.

Anna made no effort to reply.

Adonis matched her silence. Why was he speaking to a woman who never responded? Who was Anna, anyway? Or what? She appeared to be flesh and blood, but he couldn't put out of his mind the possibility that she might be a phantasm or apparition. His sense of reality might have been altered, a portion of his brain rewired prior to the transformation of his body. Anna might be no more real than the seven-headed dragon St. Michael slew in Dürer's *Apocalypse* woodcuts.

The one certainty he could get his hands around was his compulsion to reveal to someone—real or illusory—his fear that he'd become a stranger to himself. For that matter, he held doubts that he knew what his real self was—that he'd ever known. He could easily be trapped in a malicious carnival's perceptual hall of mirrors left gaping at a series of distorted images. Maybe he'd fallen through a wormhole in the universe and merged with another Adonis Licht. If so, he could only hope that the old Adonis waited for him somewhere like a shipwreck survivor clutching a life preserver while adrift in the open sea. As best he could tell, the real Adonis Licht had gone missing. He'd morphed into a brand.

"It's all so bizarre," he said. "When you're a kid, you create this fantasy you because the thing you want most is to crawl out of your skin and escape from everything people think about you. Only you end up wanting to be just like the people you can't stand." Adonis knew from experience. He'd always reviled the jocks and the cool kids—like Apollo. He'd also envied them—the alpha males with their pick of girls. Guys who got laid—or claimed they did—and went out of their way to let you know you could never do what they did, never have what they had. Guys who demolished your dreams the way construction workers jackhammered an old sidewalk into rubble and dust.

College promised a fresh start. It ended up being more like high school, but after four years, you graduated with honors while some of the cool guys barely scraped by and others never made it past freshman year—if they went to college at all. Still, nothing changed. You got a job but not a cool-guy job. You lived whatever it was you called a life. You spent a lot of time thinking about *other* people's lives.

"Then this crazy thing happens," Adonis explained. "Women look at you the way *you* used to look at *them*. You should be euphoric. Get laid every night. Only you're not and you don't. You couldn't be more confused if you woke up a thousand years from now on a different continent—a different planet. You don't know the language, you don't know the customs, you don't have a clue."

He sighed. The breath rushed out with unexpected force, a mixture of resignation and disgust. Wasn't he the Museum Man now? Wasn't the Museum Man cool by definition? So what was he doing in an alley talking to a woman covered in black plastic garbage bags? A woman who might be nothing more than a specter called to life by some deep-seated psychosis.

Still, having someone to talk with—at least, talk *to*—offered a measure of relief.

"There's this girl," he said. "This woman."

Two sharp taps on his office door drew Adonis from his post-lunch study of the scripts Aerodrome 1 had emailed. The brief, unfamiliar rhythm bore no resemblance to Fred's heavy, salsa-intonated one-to-three. He found no similarity with Mary-Louise's self-assured knock making clear the expectation that he would leap from his seat no matter how engrossing or demanding the task he currently undertook. He opened the door with the confused anticipation of a TV game show contestant.

Carla Parsont raised her hand in greeting.

"I was just talking about you this morning," Adonis said.

"With who? Or is it with whom? It's in the stylebooks, but I never seem to get it right."

"No one you'd know."

"Try me."

"Take my word."

She shrugged. "So I just finished chatting with Dr. Gelderode."

"Mary-Louise?"

"Is there another?"

Realizing that he hadn't yet invited Carla in, Adonis gestured towards his guest chair. "I thought you weren't doing anything on Mary-Louise until the fall," he said. He skirted his desk and sat.

"Jealous?"

Adonis' cheeks flushed. He would never imply disloyalty to Mary-Louise. She was his boss, and despite the awkwardness between them, his patron. "Why would I be jealous?"

"You're the Museum Man."

"That's a strange name."

"Get used to it. Your face is all over the city."

"I try not to think about it."

She arched an eyebrow. "Some of the women in the newsroom keep asking me, *What's the Museum Man like? Can you introduce me or have you staked a claim?* I half-expect they'll be asking me to pass you the keys to their apartments."

Adonis gripped the edge of his desk. He wondered if Carla was sending him a message. "I'm flattered," he said. "But this Museum Man thing... It's complicated."

She stared as if he'd addressed her in a language in which she was at best semi-fluent. "You're the only man I know who'd say that. But anyway, you know how I told you I was going to write this piece on Dr. Gelderode... Mary-Louise... for the fall? Change of plans. The powers that be want something on her for early summer. Mary-Louise is very excited. What I didn't tell her is that we have someone else in mind for the fall. For the Sunday magazine. We do profiles on major politicians and movie stars and big-time athletes. People like that. It'll run right before the Madonna and Child exhibition opens. And I get to write it."

"You can't go wrong with Hunter Kirk. He knows everyone, and everyone knows him."

"We did him a few years back. I'm talking about the Museum Man."

Adonis knew he should offer an eloquent response, gracious and, of course, humble. Only with Carla Parsont sitting across his desk, he couldn't find the words.

"To be honest," she said, "I expected more of a reaction, but then you *are* the Museum Man. Why *wouldn't* you be featured in the magazine? Anyway, sorry for barging in unannounced." She smiled. "Okay, that's a lie. About me being sorry. I'm a journalist."

Adonis considered a series of yoga breaths. Still, despite an unexpected onset of nerves, he had to put himself on the line. "I was thinking maybe we could have lunch later this week. Or dinner. A social thing."

"Not that anyone wouldn't want to go out with the Museum Man, but I'll be doing this big magazine profile on you, right? That rules out any kind of social relationship. Interviews? Sure. We can always get coffee at the café. Lunch? Dinner? Strictly business. I pay for myself then we go our separate ways after."

Adonis nodded, a bit confused but not disheartened. She had responsibilities. Limitations. He got that. But after the profile appeared in October, Carla would be freed from her vow of—what? It wasn't chastity. Fraternizing? The profile and the exhibition, however, were months off. "I hope it's going well. The interview with Mary-Louise."

She winked. "It's been very interesting."

21

O bserving that everyone else remained seated as Randolph Bennett entered the conference room, Adonis felt as exposed as the fig-leafed Adam in Titian's *Adam and Eve*. Would the others think him condescending? A sycophant? In the plain language his mother used, an ass-kisser? Or would they infer something improper in his relationship with Randolph? He wondered if, having practically leaping out of his chair, he'd unwittingly invited the people around the table to watch with malevolent glee as his awkward response stripped away the Museum Man's façade. This despite the sincere desire to demonstrate his affection for a man he respected and of whom he'd grown fond, if not in all the ways Randolph might have desired.

Randolph Bennett, flashing a warm grin, exuded the graciousness of a venerable actor making his initial entrance in a mediocre play serving as a vehicle for the launch of yet another farewell tour. He enfolded Adonis in his arms and kissed him on both cheeks.

Taken aback, Adonis imagined a first meeting with an eccentric uncle viewed by the family with continual humor and occasional scorn.

Randolph Bennett released Adonis then pinched his left cheek. Adonis' grandparents had been fond of doing that. Stepping back, he made a beckoning motion.

A woman near Adonis' age with straight brown hair framing broad cheeks verging on sallow stepped forward. She carried a laptop and a black leather portfolio.

Adonis conferred on her a five.

"Let me introduce my Assistant Curator, Mona Pavlic," said Randolph Bennett. "Adonis and Mona have been in contact for some time now."

Mona Pavlic extended her hand. "It's wonderful to finally meet you, Adonis."

"And you," Adonis returned. He noted the contrast between her warm voice and her hand, which she might have just withdrawn from an ice-filled beer chest.

Randolph Bennett tilted his head.

Mona Pavlic sat.

Randolph Bennett turned to Hunter Kirk, settled in his customary spot at the head of the table, eyes shifting from his guest to his watch and back again. "Breakfast this morning was lovely, Hunter. Thank you." In turn he smiled at Tyler Severinsen and Mary-Louise Gelderode. Then he shifted his attention to the other end of the table. An easel devoid of anything to exhibit stood at its edge.

Adonis detected puzzlement on the faces around the table—all but Mona Pavlic's.

Randolph Bennett turned back to his hosts. "Pardon my rather effusive greeting for Adonis, but at the risk of an embarrassing exaggeration, much of the American public... certainly those with a taste for art and culture... seems to have fallen in love with the Museum Man." He raised his right hand to his heart. "You understand, Adonis, that I am not suggesting anything that is not professional and, by inference, unnatural."

The room erupted in laughter.

Adonis joined in.

Randolph Bennett motioned Adonis to sit then stood behind his own seat.

Hunter Kirk released an audible sigh. "This visit, Randolph. You've left us in the dark."

Randolph Bennett gestured towards Mona Pavlic. "*Our visit concerns The Madonna of the Heavenly Palace.* Ms. Pavlic and I have returned it as promised."

Hunter Kirk stroked his beard. "We appreciate that, Randolph. But you weren't expected to bring it back personally." He tapped his watch.

"Hunter, you bond the heart of an artist with the soul of an accountant. If accountants have souls. However, I thought a meeting quite essential." He waved towards the open door leading to the hallway.

Two museum employees carried in a rectangular object swaddled in protective wrapping and placed it on the easel.

Randolph Bennett signaled them to exit. "And do be so kind as to close the door."

Mona Pavlic removed the wrapping then retook her seat.

"*The Madonna of the Heavenly Palace,*" said Randolph Bennett, as if beginning a familiar yet anticipated soliloquy. "The very same masterwork by the renowned Norbertus of Hannover graciously entrusted by you to my institution." He motioned to Adonis. "Adonis, you are probably more familiar with this painting than anyone in this room. Would you be so kind as to verify that this is, indeed, the same work you shipped to us."

Adonis looked at Mary-Louise.

Mary-Louise looked at Hunter Kirk.

Hunter Kirk nodded.

Adonis approached the painting. He recognized not only the masterly combination of bright and dark colors but also the technique—uncommonly bold brush strokes and highlights featuring thick opaque paint mixed with generous amounts of white lead pigment. "Yes," he said. "This is the painting."

"There you have it from our very own Adonis," said Randolph Bennett, "and if anyone in the art world is to be believed, it is he. As an aside, Hunter, you can be assured of the success of your new fundraising campaign featuring the Museum Man."

Tyler Severinsen coughed into his hand as Adonis returned to his seat. "Randolph, you weren't out drinking last night, were you?"

"A bottle of wine with dinner, Tyler. A *shared* bottle of wine and no more." He shrugged. "Perhaps an after-dinner brandy, but only one. I *think* one."

Mary-Louise smiled. "Honestly, Randolph, did you think we'd send you a fake?"

Randolph Bennett squinted. "Of course not." He took an actor's beat pause. "But you *did.*"

Adonis' heart pounded like a blacksmith's hammer pummeling red-hot iron on an anvil.

Hunter Kirk stared ahead then erupted in laughter. "Jesus, Randolph! You almost had me believing you. It's all those damn plays you acted in at Oxford. You should have gone on to the Royal Shakespeare Company or the West End."

Tyler Severinsen and Mary-Louise chuckled, relieved that Hunter Kirk had broken the tension.

Despite the mirth exhibited around the table, Adonis remained puzzled by Randolph's droll performance. He and Fred had done the provenance. The senior chain of command had approved their report. And what about Clark Merrill? He was a sophisticated collector, not some boob emerging from the hinterlands with the tale of a painting bestowed by a maiden aunt who'd purchased a pleasant piece of art from a rickety stall on the banks of the Seine or one of Amsterdam's canals. A forgery? A fraud? A fake? No one in Randolph Bennett's position could possibly find that material for humor.

Randolph Bennett pointed at Adonis. "Now *there* is a man who understands the gravity of the situation."

Adonis gripped the armrests of his chair. What was Randolph implying? Or, having been rebuffed the night they met, was Randolph taking his revenge served cold by rendering Adonis momentarily discomfited?

Hunter Kirk scowled. "Don't fuck with me, Randolph."

Tyler Severinsen and Mary-Louise both blanched.

The last traces of affability in Randolph Bennett's face melted away. "Mona?"

Mona Pavlic distributed copies of a large, folded document.

Adonis noted an architect's plan for the renovation of the exterior of a palace now more familiar than that of his apartment building.

Mona Pavlic approached the painting. "It's a phenomenal effort, honestly, but still a fake. And we owe it all to Adonis."

Heads turned.

Adonis fought to hold up his own.

"The palace," she said. "That was the tip-off."

Adonis leaned forward so that his body language would convey an image blending integrity and innocence. Besides, he had nothing to hide. He had only assisted Mary-Louise in supporting the Museum's acquisition of a gift everyone welcomed. Now, it seemed that his job—his career—might be on the line. Unless there was some mistake. But an eminence like Randolph Bennett would never call a meeting like this unless he could substantiate his accusation. Someone, as they said in gangster movies, would have to take the fall.

"So Adonis and I have had this ongoing exchange of information regarding documents and papers about

Norbertus," Mona Pavlic explained. "About Cardinal Giordano, too." Many of those documents had been discovered or released only in recent months. Her people had unearthed architectural drawings of proposed renovations to the exterior of the Palazzo Giordano. Fire damaged the palazzo in 1576. "This, of course, is the palace in our painting. But look at the lower right corner of the drawing."

The architect's plan bore the date 1594.

"Cardinal Giordano obviously wants to spiff up the palace," she said. "The architect adds more windows to the two upper floors and changes the detailing at their tops, alternating arch-and-point pediments all the way across. He definitely rips off Michelangelo." The architect also added elaboration to the corners of the building and around the arched entry. "Personally, I think he makes the palazzo look more like an office building, but we're caretakers and interpreters of art, not critics. What's relevant is, this plan was drawn eleven years *after* Norbertus' death."

Additional research attested that work on the palazzo was completed in 1596. The new windows and elaborations all appeared in the painting. "To be honest, I didn't even notice until a few days after the painting arrived. You look at a work of art and everything's wonderful and then something just hits you and you don't know why but you see things in a whole new light. I went back to the architect's drawings. Norbertus never could have painted this piece."

Mary-Louise stood. "The piece was examined by experts."

Hunter Kirk motioned her to sit. "This architectural drawing," he asked. "You've had it authenticated? It's not misdated?"

"Authenticated, Dr. Kirk? Yes. Misdated? Not likely."

"Unless," said Mary-Louise, "the architect or some predecessor drew up those plans after the fire but still during Norbertus' lifetime. Norbertus could have seen them and painted the palace as it was going to be."

Hunter Kirk looked at Adonis.

Adonis cleared his throat. "Drafting a copy of the original plans wouldn't be out of the question. Cardinal Giordano suffered several financial setbacks. He could have delayed the project for years then had new copies made if the old plans were partially damaged in the same fire at the palazzo that destroyed Norbertus' paintings."

Tyler Severinsen's fingertips tapped lightly on the table. "We're in an awkward position here. I don't want to say, Ms. Pavlic... and to you, Randolph... that you're jumping to an unwarranted conclusion. But Adonis' point is well taken. Of course, we'll have the painting tested. But it's going to be difficult to distinguish some of the technical details, like pigments and oils mixed in say 1598 and... what's the date of record for this painting?"

"Fifteen eighty-two," Adonis answered.

"Let's also consider the palette and brush strokes. They obviously didn't arouse the suspicions of the consultants we called in."

Like a director blocking a scene in rehearsal, Randolph Bennett motioned Mona Pavlic to return to her seat. "Are you suggesting, Tyler, the possibility of a fake by one of Norbertus' students after his death? Perhaps someone copied Norbertus' original painting that later was destroyed or disappeared. Or someone went through Norbertus' files after his death and worked from one of his studies."

"*You're* suggesting all that, Randolph, not me."

"Tyler, I am not suggesting the involvement of a student or an associate at all."

Hunter Kirk slammed the table with his fist. Mugs and glasses clattered. "Shit, Randolph. You had the painting tested."

A wave of heat rocketed from Adonis' stomach up to his chest and enflamed his cheeks.

"*Our* people tested the painting," said Hunter Kirk.

"Your lab is excellent, Hunter, really. Perhaps our equipment and software happen to be a bit more up to date. Or your technicians had a bad day. Precedents abound. At any rate, this painting... quite an exquisite piece, really... is an early-twentieth-century work. Probably pre-War. The war to make the world safe for democracy, as your President Wilson termed it. The work of someone highly skilled. Han van Meegeren comes to mind, although he specialized in Vermeers. Icilio Joni's name might appear on a list of suspects. If not, someone possessing similar talent and cleverness, which is saying quite a lot."

"And you had what done? X-ray diffraction?"

"Which revealed that the artist... and he *was* an artist in his own right... used zinc white."

"A nineteenth-century invention," said Adonis.

Randolph Bennett nodded. "We did X-ray fluorescence, as well."

The forger, Mona Pavlic related, was an accomplished chemist, but the pigments were too pure. As to the craquelure, that also was handled with care. The painting was probably baked at low heat a year or more after it was finished. In sum, the forger knew that Norbertus had created a painting with a palace floating in the sky. Cardinal Giordano's palace. Fortunately for the forger, no one had seen the painting in over a hundred years. The faux Norbertus probably sketched the palazzo in Rome or saw an image in a book and thus never concerned himself with the possibility of a renovation following Norbertus' death. Or he knew of the renovation but wagered that no one would match its date with that of the painting.

Randolph Bennett approached Adonis. "And here, the Museum Man's thesis comes into play. The architectural drawings we have for the renovation could well have been copies of originals lost in that unfortunate conflagration." He held his hand out.

Mona Pavlic withdrew another set of documents. "The test results."

Mary-Louise slumped in her seat, as doleful as the Mary memorialized by Michelangelo's *Pietà*.

Hunter Kirk rose from his chair and stood behind Mary-Louise.

Adonis feared that Hunter would deliver the coup-de-grace right in front of them.

Hunter Kirk rested his hands on Mary-Louise's shoulders. Inches from her neck, Adonis considered.

"Forgeries, fakes," said Hunter Kirk. "There isn't a major museum in the world that hasn't been fooled. Or a connoisseur whose reputation no one had the guts to challenge until someone else proved him wrong. Remember Bernard Berenson claiming that Titian painted the *Allendale Nativity*? Later the painting was attributed to Giorgione." He rubbed Mary-Louise's shoulders like a trainer preparing a fighter to enter the ring. "Not to be crass, but shit happens."

"Not on my watch," said Mary-Louise.

"On *your* watch?" Hunter Kirk responded. "On *my* watch. On *all* our watches." He withdrew his hands. "Shit happens and shit stinks, and we move on. We'll review the lab reports, but we'll also jump on developing a strategy for handling this revelation and quick. I'll speak with Lenore Josephson. We'll bring in a consultant on crisis management. We'll figure a way to spin this. Cover our asses and move forward."

"Ah," said Randolph Bennett, "the show must go on. Thank goodness there is no question about the provenance of any of the other Madonna and Child pieces."

Adonis shot to his feet. "The exhibition will be better than ever."

Heads swiveled.

Adonis had no idea what compelled him to offer a response—particularly *that* response. But having committed himself—or some unknown and unbidden force having committed him—he continued. "There's been so much media coverage about Norbertus. So much excitement. But we face an ongoing challenge. How to sustain it. Our Norbertus a fake? The Museum couldn't dream up a bigger story.

"Being fooled," said Hunter Kirk, "is not the kind of news we like to broadcast."

Adonis placed his hands on the table while holding to his position as if he was rooted to the spot. If Hunter was going to fire him after the meeting, he might as well let loose. Not that he didn't fear for his prospects—if he *had* prospects. "*Exactly* the news we'd like to broadcast," he insisted.

The Museum had to make an announcement. That was a given. If they then buried the fake in some storeroom or vault, they'd look foolish. They didn't have to. An old saying came into play. There's no such thing as bad publicity. Beyond that, bad publicity could be turned into *good* publicity.

"As Dr. Kirk just said," Adonis wound up, "things happen."

"As I recall," said Hunter Kirk, "and I *do* recall, I said *shit* happens." He motioned Adonis to continue.

"We don't bury the fake. We *celebrate* it. We still make it the centerpiece of the exhibition, only we tell the story behind a remarkable fake that fooled so many of us. We display the architectural drawings we found. *Mona* found. We display the lab tests. Show people the science. And we show visitors *how* the piece was faked. How forgers... honestly, they're artists in their own right... create pigments and oils and even find old boards and frames. We still have a room devoted to Norbertus, but we turn it into an exhibition about fakes and forgeries. A show within a show." He glanced at Randolph Bennett. "Like Hamlet's play within a play. One about saints and sinners. Norbertus comes off as a saint, but what really draws visitors is sin."

Tyler Severinsen held his hands up, palms pressed against each other in a gesture intimating prayer.

Adonis swallowed. He'd heard the words as he'd spoken them as if he'd stepped out of his body. They seemed to have made sense. But how could he have been so impulsive, taken that kind of risk? Yes, the Museum would announce that it had been had. That Clark Merrill had been had. But trumpet a fake? He'd just told his superiors, some of the most respected people in the profession, that they should make a game of a disaster. Was he rubbing their noses in... well, shit?

"We have a lot to think about," said Hunter Kirk. "Tyler, you and I will speak with Lenore and Julia Edelstein. Get some perspective on how this might impact Development. We'll anticipate what fires to put out and how. When we're ready, I'll call a meeting of the Board. Mary-Louise and I will inform Clark Merrill before that."

"Speaking with Clark," said Mary-Louise, "won't be pleasant."

"Because we fucked up? And *he* fucked up? Damn right it won't be pleasant. But we'll deal with it. That includes sitting down with our corporate sponsors, and you can bet your ass I'm not looking forward to *that*." Hunter Kirk turned to Randolph Bennett. "Randolph, you need to explain things on your end. On a need-to-know basis, of course."

"I'm not sure if this matter will be taken with indignation or bemusement," Randolph Bennett said. "Do be assured, though, that I will enlighten our board and senior staff. I assume we'll make some sort of joint announcement."

"Yes, but only after we examine the situation from every angle. As far as Adonis' suggestion..." Hunter Kirk looked at his watch. "People, we have work to do."

Mary-Louise stared at the table.

It seemed to Adonis that she'd suddenly withered from a ten to a six—even a five—like a fairytale princess cast under a spell by a wicked witch.

As to his own status, Adonis couldn't help believing that he now teetered on a high wire twenty, thirty, a hundred stories in the air. Tyler hadn't offered the least measure of encouragement. Hunter's response indicated no reason for optimism. And Mary-Louise? At best, she was trying to determine which way the wind was blowing.

Randolph Bennett might have tilted the scales in his favor, but Adonis now interpreted his displays of affection as the polished mannerisms of an actor skilled at charming museum donors rather than theater audiences. The meeting had been a set-up. Randolph could have called Hunter and emailed the documents. Instead, he'd flown in to watch the Museum Man squirm, paying out just enough rope to leave Adonis dangling. Like a fool, Adonis had tightened the knot around his neck then released the trap door beneath his own feet. He had it coming. He'd flaunted the Museum's failure. *His* failure. No doubt everyone in the room had come to the same conclusion: Adonis Licht, like *The Madonna of the Heavenly Palace*, was a fake.

Sleep evaded Adonis that night even if the remainder of his day had proved uneventful. Of course, he never mentioned the forgery to Fred. Hunter Kirk laid down the law. The matter was to be kept as secret as the nuclear Manhattan Project during World War Two. At home, he prepared a mainstay dinner of chicken and vegetables, but as soon as he sat down, his appetite vanished. He poured a rare glass of wine. He wished he had a joint, although he'd smoked pot fewer than half-a-dozen times, the last in graduate school. Towards midnight, he thought of calling Carla Parsont but feared he'd irritate her. Worse, she'd hear the concern in his voice, launch a probe and discover the skeleton in the Museum's closet before the making of the joint announcement. In bed, he listened to Dvorak's *New World Symphony* distracted by the nagging realization that the other shoe hovered. In time, it would drop. He'd be dispatched with a figurative bullet to the head, his career dumped into the museum world's equivalent of an unmarked grave. The only question was who would pull the trigger.

Restless, Adonis slipped on a pair of jeans and cross-trainers, and fled to the streets. He encountered a trickle of people returning home from a late shift at a restaurant or convenience store, or calling it quits after closing a bar or leaving a party that might or might not last until dawn. A stream of buses, taxis, automobiles and trucks—reduced from their daytime numbers but remarkably constant—maintained the pulse of a city slowed by the early-morning hour but by no means brought to a standstill. He stopped to get his bearings.

Footsteps sounded. Half a block ahead, two men approached. One erupted into laughter. The other offered a muffled response.

Adonis considered crossing the street but reasoned that appearing to flee would convey fear and vulnerability. He continued walking forward, careful to keep his pace steady and determined. This, he reasoned, would communicate the self-assurance of a man best left unbothered. Besides, they'd have to take on a man become a grotesque freakily strong.

The men drew closer. Their conversation ceased.

Adonis balled his fists. His chest felt constricted as if a mugger twice his size had leaped from the shadows and wrapped him in a bear hug.

The men passed without looking at him. Their footsteps faded.

Sotto voce, Adonis recited the oft-quoted line from F. Scott Fitzgerald's *The Crack-up*: "In a real dark night of the soul it is always three o'clock in the morning." He stopped beneath a streetlight.

A silver stretch limousine approached.

He turned toward it.

The limousine slowed. An attractive young woman with long blonde hair, her arms raised, emerged through the sunroof like an old-time striptease dancer popping up out of a giant birthday cake. She blew a kiss. Then, as the limo passed, she descended like a mermaid, wary of lingering on land, slipping back into the sea.

Adonis leaned against the lamppost. He wondered if the woman had mocked him as another of those lonely men who wandered the city at odd hours. Which he was. A sputtering neon sign across the street drew his attention. It went in and out of focus. He placed his hand over his heart.

Lights flashed.

Adonis closed his eyes.

A car door opened and closed. More footsteps sounded. A hand gripped his shoulder.

Adonis opened his eyes.

A police officer studied him. Broad-shouldered with close-cut hair, he wore gold-rimmed glasses. Emerging jowls marked a young face turning fleshy.

Adonis placed the tip of his left index finger against his left nostril and took a yoga breath. Then he switched to the right.

"You okay, sir?" the officer asked.

Adonis dropped his hand.

"You okay?" the officer repeated.

Adonis remained silent. Wasn't there something in the law about having the right to do that?

"Sir, please touch your finger to your nose again, please," said the officer. His voice blended concern with professional wariness.

Adonis left his hands at his side.

"Do you have any history of medical problems? Seizures? Anything like that, sir?"

Adonis took a deep mouth breath and exhaled slowly. "No. I'm fine." He straightened, hoping that an approximation of good posture would satisfy the officer's curiosity.

"Sir, do you live around here, sir?" the officer asked.

Adonis felt oddly distanced from himself. "I don't think so," he said.

"You don't think so?"

"Not all that close, I don't think."

The officer sniffed then peered into his eyes. "Have you been drinking, sir? Smoking anything?"

"No. Honest."

The officer nodded his assent. "Medications? You take any medications?"

"No."

"And you don't live around here?"

"No."

"May I please see some identification, please, sir?"

"Identification?"

The officer moved his right hand to the radio at his left shoulder. "Driver's license. ID card. You understand that a police officer has the right to ask someone for identification?"

Adonis nodded.

"May I see your identification, sir?"

Adonis reached into his right-front pocket.

"Slowly, please."

He took out his wallet and opened it with his driver's license displayed.

"Please take it out of the wallet," said the officer. "Your license, please."

Adonis took another deep breath. His head began to clear.

The officer shined a flashlight on the license. "What's your name, sir, please?"

"Adonis. Licht."

The officer looked up at Adonis then back down to the driver's license. "When did you renew your license?"

"Last year."

"They take a new photo then?"

"I think so."

"So this is a recent photo?"

"Yes."

"It's not you." The officer's voice betrayed a slight edge. "You know that, don't you?"

"I got sick a while ago. I lost weight. A lot of weight. Now I go to the gym. I don't look like that anymore."

The officer examined the license again. "Adonis Licht," he said. "Really?" His head snapped up. He handed the wallet back to Adonis. "It's a little late to be out by yourself, Mr. Licht."

"I couldn't sleep."

"I'll be glad to give you a lift home."

"I'm fine. Really. I'm fine now. And I like to walk late at night."

The officer ran his tongue along the inside of his left cheek. "It's not illegal to walk around the city at this hour, but maybe it's not the smartest thing you can do. You sure you don't want a ride?"

"No. Thank you. That's very kind, but I'll head home in a minute."

The officer shrugged. "Your choice, Mr. Licht. Just please look out for yourself, please."

"Certainly," said Adonis. "Absolutely."

The officer winked. "Can't have anything happen to the Museum Man."

22

is world imploding, Adonis spent the weekend in his apartment. Adding to his doldrums, approaching summer brought with it weather turned warm and muggy. The fan stationed between the foot of the bed and the sofa stirred a stream of air Adonis could acknowledge only as indolent.

Late Sunday evening, despite the heat, he stood in the kitchen preparing to broil a piece of salmon. As he unwrapped the package, he continued trying to digest Randolph Bennett's revelation and steel himself for the recriminations his superiors would direct his way once they finished letting him twist in the wind.

Oddly, an illusory measure of normalcy prevailed at the Museum. Adonis—to all intents occupied with the varied and grave responsibilities his new position entailed—kept his office door closed. Half his time he devoted to the Madonna and Child exhibition. The other half he spent scouring the internet for job postings and the possibilities of finding work in related fields.

Fred aside, the staff left Adonis undisturbed. Mary-Louise held herself aloof. Adonis assumed she was engaged in crucial conversations with Tyler Severinsen and Hunter Kirk. Doubtless, their exchanges included his future at the Museum. Or lack of one. He couldn't imagine Mary-Louise supporting him. Not that her advocacy would make a difference. Sooner or later, the Museum would terminate him. The only matter in need of clarification regarded whether they would grant him a stay of execution until the exhibition closed. Exoneration represented nothing more than a delusion.

Having again regurgitated the week—over the past forty-eight hours, he'd done it too many times to count—he placed the rinsed salmon into a pan. Back at the fridge, he removed Swiss chard for steaming. His cell, left on the coffee table, interrupted him. He stood for a moment in front of the open refrigerator letting the cold air refresh him until the cell went quiet. After setting the chard on the counter, he shambled to the coffee table, picked up the cell and clicked on voicemail. His heart fluttered like the wings of a game bird shot down in flight.

Hunter Kirk wanted him in his office the next morning. Early.

As the sky lightened, Adonis put on the oversize sport coat he'd bought online, grabbed his sunglasses and put on the straw fedora with the wide brim he'd recently purchased then rushed to the gym for a truncated workout. He intended to enjoy his membership before he had to cancel it. He also planned to trim his other expenses to stretch his severance pay. Assuming he would be given a severance. His unemployment payments would go only so far. Assuming he'd be eligible to collect unemployment. He contemplated searching out Anna after leaving the gym so that her unspoken support might strengthen him for the meeting with Hunter. More realistically, Dr. Kirk. He doubted they remained on a first-name basis.

Despite the best of intentions, he found himself running late heading out of the gym. Dr. Kirk expected him at seven-thirty. That left no time to find Anna. He weighed the consequences of showing up late. What more could Dr. Kirk do than fire him for insubordination? Although that might cost him his unemployment payments. On the other hand, humility seemed a better strategy. If he appeared contrite, Dr. Kirk might forego any form of reprisal. Dr. Kirk might even offer to have Tyler—Dr. Severinsen—or Mary-Louise provide a reference letter. No matter how bland, it would impress some mediocre museum in some mediocre city with a budget as limited as its horizons.

Determined to meet his end with a measure of grace and equanimity, Adonis jogged. He stopped as he reached the plaza in front of the Museum. As his body shed heat, a flock of pigeons swirled overhead like a kaleidoscopic storm cloud then settled on the ledges high above the entry doors.

After greeting the security guard at the employee entrance and exchanging a few innocuous words about the warm weather and the likelihood that he would star in his own reality show before the year was out, Adonis checked his cell. It showed seven twenty-two. Satisfied that he'd made the effort to comply with Dr. Kirk's instructions but seeing no point in sprinting to the chopping block, he walked towards his office. He'd make a sixty-second determination—*triage* would be an appropriate term—as to which of his personal items to take home, which to trash and which to give further consideration.

Two steps past Mary-Louise's door, he spun on his heels. Where was her nameplate? The naked patch where it had been—slightly darker than the surrounding area—revealed only two screw holes as vacant as Mary-Louise's eyes after Mona Pavlic announced the Norbertus fakery. His eyes lingered on the holes, which suggested the puncture wound of giant snake in a Hollywood horror flick. He tried the knob. It resisted. Admittedly, he found nothing odd there. Mary-Louise kept her door locked when she was out, and she never came to the office this early. But her nameplate? His cell displayed seven twenty-eight. He ran to the hallway and leaped up the stairs to the executive offices.

Dr. Kirk's door was open.

Adonis knocked anyway.

"Punctual to the minute," Dr. Kirk sang out as if he'd beckoned Adonis to share a little buddy time before starting work.

Hat in hand, Adonis remained in the doorway and stared.

Books and papers littered the massive surface of an eighteenth-century oak dining table from a chateau in the Loire River Valley.

Dr. Kirk stared back at Adonis. "You find that jacket in a thrift shop or what? Or is baggy back in style? If you wear it, it must be. And nice hat." He tapped his head.

Adonis put on the hat, counted to three, removed it then stepped forward. He spotted Dr. Severinsen standing to Dr. Kirk's right.

"Good morning," Dr. Severinsen said. He smiled as if he looked forward to a casual update on a restoration or a flier promoting a new lecture.

Adonis hadn't expected Dr. Severinsen, although his presence shouldn't have come as a surprise. The Chief Curator might not wish to miss the bloodletting. Unlike his mother, whose emotions could literally be taken at face value, these two men effortlessly concealed their cold-blooded intent. Most likely, they considered this an amusement, a matter to be recounted over lunch or evening drinks and met with jaded laughter. Resigned to his fate, Adonis nodded in deference then glanced around the office like a condemned man—St. Thomas More came to mind—embracing one last sunrise.

Only the final shuffling to the executioner's block awaiting, Adonis reflected that he'd never been in Dr. Kirk's office. Its size startled him. Presidents of giant corporations, he imagined, made weighty decisions from offices like this. Why not Dr. Kirk? His primary function consisted of currying favor with powerful CEOs, as well as wealthy patrons, corporate sponsors, politicians and major players in the art world.

Adonis glanced at the large window overlooking the plaza at the Museum's main entrance. In front of the window stood a leather sofa and several armchairs in mocha brown, furnishings appropriate in a prestigious alumni club. His eyes wandered to floor-standing sculptures from the Museum's various collections. Smaller works occupied nooks and shelves. Paintings and drawings covered the walls. He recognized a watercolor by Hans Hoffmann—not the twentieth-century abstract expressionist but the German Mannerist, a contemporary of Norbertus. He'd included it in a small exhibition he'd curated the year before last. Behind Dr. Kirk stood more shelves filled with books, binders and—

"That's one hell of a special football," said Dr. Kirk. He rose and walked Adonis to a leather sofa.

Dr. Severinsen joined them.

"People always seem so startled," said Dr. Kirk. "Or they think, *Well, sure. All black men play sports.*" A second-string tight end during his senior year, he'd caught the winning touchdown against his school's archrival with seventeen seconds left. "Division Three ball. No pro scouts in the stands. Well, maybe one or two but not to see me. It was my only touchdown of the season. If you must know, of my career. A broken play. Life's all about timing." And discipline, he pointed out. It took discipline to earn a Ph.D. and an MBA. "No easy task for your average street kid." He chuckled. "Of course, my father was a corporate lawyer, and my mother was a pediatrician." He placed a hand on Adonis' shoulder. "You play football?" he asked, exhibiting no memory of Adonis' previous self.

"No, sir."

He slid his hand up towards Adonis' neck then clapped him on the back. "You would have punished people."

Adonis shivered.

"Had coffee?" Dr. Kirk asked. "I hope so, because my admin brews it before the café opens, but I told her not to come in until eight. And Tyler's no use."

"My admin *never* comes in until eight-*thirty*," said Dr. Severinsen. "But Hunter, as everyone knows, is a hard-ass."

Adonis found it odd—cruel, really—hearing these two men trade banter like a late-night talk-show host and his genial sidekick. But no display of affability could conceal that they were about to initiate the crash-and-burn phase of his career.

"You understand," said Dr. Kirk, "we want to speak with you privately."

Dr. Severinsen grimaced. "This whole matter... Terribly unfortunate. Painful. Really, I wish the situation was otherwise. We both do."

The blood drained from Adonis' cheeks.

"Give it some perspective, son. What choice did we have? We *had* to let Dr. Gelderode go."

Adonis stood immobile, processing what he'd just heard. "Dr. Gelderode? Because the Norbertus was a fake?"

Dr. Kirk scratched the underside of his bearded jaw. "That? Hell no. Obviously, no one's happy about a fake showing up on the Museum's doorstep, but fakes and forgeries are nothing new in the art world. Galleries and auction houses fall for them all the time. Museums, too. I'm sure you know the history as well as I do." He patted Adonis on the knee like a coach comforting a player who'd fumbled on his own one-yard line but would go back out on the field when his team next had the ball and give his all. "No, it wasn't the fake." He looked at Adonis for a moment then asked, "You know that reporter..."

"Carla Parsont," said Dr. Severinsen.

Adonis nodded.

"What happened was," Hunter Kirk continued, "Ms. Parsont called me Friday morning."

"Very attractive young lady," said Dr. Severinsen.

Dr. Kirk winked. "She told me she was doing something on Mary-Louise. And that upcoming magazine profile on you."

Adonis clasped his hands to keep them from shaking. Had Carla found out that he and Mary-Louise had spent a night together? One single night? Had that violated some clause in Mary-Louise's employment contract? He'd never seen a stipulation regarding sex with a fellow employee or manager in his own agreement.

He concluded that the matter involved something more. They were leading him on, waiting for him to condemn himself with some offhand comment about Mary-Louise or the fake about which they seemed so dismissive. Conceivably, Mary-Louise had entangled herself in an entirely different matter, and they found him guilty by association. He was— had been until this morning—one of Mary-Louise's people. She hired him. She promoted him. He couldn't avoid circling back to the fake Norbertus. He'd done the provenance. His name equated with fingerprints on a knife at a murder scene.

"Here's the thing," said Dr. Kirk, "Ms. Parsont wanted me to comment on a story her newspaper plans to break tomorrow."

Adonis found himself lost again.

"Somehow, Ms. Parsont discovered that Dr. Gelderode spent a long weekend in the Bahamas."

"The Bahamas?" Adonis asked in total confusion. Dr. Kirk seemed to be tossing non-sequiturs like a flower girl scattering rose petals at a wedding.

Dr. Kirk laughed. "Damn, son, I really don't care where my employees take their vacations. Me? I love the Bahamas. You, Tyler?"

"Wonderful place, the Bahamas."

"The problem is, Dr. Gelderode went to the Bahamas with Clark Merrill."

Adonis' eyes widened. He recalled Mary-Louise being away while he was sick and the straw handbag in her office.

"Social media can bite you in the ass," said Dr. Kirk. "As to how Ms. Parsont got the photos she showed me, she wouldn't say. But she also had documentation concerning the villa where they stayed. Beautiful pool. A cook. A Rolls and a driver."

"And Mary-Louise," Adonis asked. "She did that to acquire the Norbertus?"

Dr. Kirk shrugged. "Things get complicated between men and women. Ask my wife. Hell, ask my ex."

"Naturally, we spoke with Dr. Gelderode," said Dr. Severinsen.

Dr. Kirk shook his head. "Not that I want to be unkind or crude, but in answer to your question, no small number of people are going to think Dr. Gelderode prostituted herself to secure the Norbertus. And by implication that the Museum encourages that sort of behavior. Or at least condones it. I mean, really... Fucking a board member? A married man at that?" He sighed. "I give Mary-Louise *this*. She fell on her sword. Just apologized, went back to her office and wrote her letter of resignation."

"This will end her career," Adonis said.

Dr. Kirk glanced at Dr. Severinsen then back to Adonis. "Mary-Louise will land somewhere. But let's talk about *you*."

Adonis froze.

"Based on similar experiences," said Dr. Severinsen. "Hunter and I agree... and so does Lenore Josephson... that this matter will burn itself out fairly quickly. At least as far as the public is concerned."

Clark Merrill would keep a low profile and resign his board seat. In a few days, weeks at most, a terrorist attack somewhere or an outrageous declaration by a politician in Washington would divert any residue of negative attention from the public's fleeting awareness. Insiders would chew on the matter, but they'd eventually grow bored and seek out new opportunities for dishing copious amounts of dirt. "Not much to do but hold our heads high. No need to supply oxygen for the fire."

Damage control was already being plotted. In a week, the Museum would announce its discovery of the fake. A few board members likely would foam at the mouth, but the Museum hierarchy could take the heat. "Mary-Louise's being responsible for the Norbertus acquisition will deflect all but the most hard-assed criticism. A week later, we'll announce our exhibition within the exhibition... a great story about fakes featuring our very own faux *Madonna of the Heavenly Palace*."

Adonis thought he saw the clouds part.

Dr. Kirk stood. "Let this be a lesson, son. The first thing you do when you have a problem? You own up from the get-go. Makes you almost look like a hero. And when you can point a finger..." He beckoned Adonis to stand.

Adonis experienced an almost palpable sensation of the executioner's blade caressing his neck. After all the affability, all the diversions, he was about to be bled, butchered and burned to make atonement. He glanced out the window. Two pigeons—mates?—glided by.

Dr. Kirk put his arm around Adonis. "Of course, we have another card to play. Someone we'll put out front on all this. Someone to help us bleach out the shit stains."

23

Less than a block from the Museum on a walk to absorb the reassurances Hunter Kirk—Hunter—had just made, Adonis heard a siren. He froze. The siren grew louder, its pitch higher. His vision dimmed. His breath grew short. He bent over and rested his hands on his knees. Pedestrians hurried by. He waited, panting.

The siren's scream receded beneath the din of Monday-morning morning traffic. Adonis straightened.

He wondered if he'd experienced a visceral reaction to a tragedy of which he had no knowledge, one that would transform—if not end—the life of someone with whom he had no acquaintance. He dismissed the thought. He'd long believed he'd become desensitized to urban life's daily calamities. He raised a hand to the back of his neck as if to shield it from an unseen assailant then lowered it. More likely, he reasoned, he'd suffered a delayed response to the fears he'd brought to the meeting with Hunter and Tyler.

Walking on to his favorite café, Adonis indulged in a flight of fancy. He imagined himself an undercover police officer or a foreign agent in a low-budget movie. The broad brim of his hat hid his forehead. Sunglasses concealed his eyes. The sport coat Hunter had called out made him look more like the old, bulky Adonis Licht. He found it reasonable to believe that the modest disguise gave him almost superhero powers to go about unseen.

Still free of intrusive admirers after leaving the café, he took away a cardboard tray with two lattes and two apple turnovers. Although he faced a challenging day given his expanded duties since he'd have to assume some of Mary-Louise's workload, he could no longer delay sharing a few minutes with Anna.

Adonis approached the alley.

Anna sat beside her grocery cart.

He placed the tray at her feet.

Her eyes accepted his offering.

Adonis picked up the paper bag containing his turnover. He had arrived at the conviction that his diet, like his workouts, made no impact on his physical condition. His meticulous regimen served only to veil an inescapable truth both from others and himself. The Museum Man was an aberration—the construct of some cosmic Dr. Frankenstein, who had refashioned his bones, flesh, muscles, sinews and organs while eviscerating the core of his being.

Anna picked up her latte and held it, waiting as always for him to leave before she consumed his gift.

Adonis stuffed his turnover into his mouth.

Fred, wide-eyed in Adonis' doorway, pointed towards Mary-Louise's vacated office. His hand exhibited a slight tremor.

Adonis nodded. "I got in early then I went out for coffee."

"Did you know before that?"

"Before I came to the Museum this morning?"

"Your buddies upstairs. Assuming they're *still* your buddies. They didn't give you a heads-up over the weekend?"

"No, I got the same email this morning you did." Adonis saw no reason to reveal his earlier meeting with Hunter and Tyler. Fred would assume they'd told him why Mary-Louise was gone and stay on his case all day until the story broke online. Not that Adonis would say anything even after the story broke. If the fake Norbertus hadn't given Hunter and Tyler enough reason to let him go, compromising what they'd divulged would afford them more than enough motive.

Fred's eyes narrowed. "She resigned just like that and no one's saying anything until the Museum releases a statement? That doesn't bother you?"

"Waiting for the statement?"

"Mary-Louise walks out. Someone should be telling us something."

"They emailed what the emailed. If you want to know more, talk to the people upstairs."

"Like that'll do any good. And anyway, where does that leave *us*?"

Adonis sighed. As if being in on the secret wasn't enough, he had secrets of his own. "As far as Mary-Louise goes," he said, "she hired me. She promoted me. So yes, her leaving bothers me. As far as what happens next, I don't know anything more than you. So let's just wait and see how this plays out."

"She didn't tell you then," said Fred.

"Tell me what?"

"That something was going on."

"Like what?"

"A hint. Maybe she dropped a hint last week?"

"No. Nothing. I'm as surprised as you are."

Fred scratched the back of his head, signaling that he'd concluded his line of questioning. "There's a snowball's chance in hell the new Curator in Charge will be anything approaching a ten."

"You're assuming they'll hire another woman."

"Another Mary-Louise couldn't hurt. Jesus, I'd give my right nut to spend a night with a woman like that. Hell, an hour."

"Your right nut? It would be worth it?"

"Easy for you to be blasé. You attract tens like a magnet draws paper clips. For the rest of us..." He pointed to the wide-brimmed hat on top of the bookcase that crowded Adonis' desk. "New?"

Adonis turned. "The hat? Yes."

"Nice. Although you could hide a mariachi band under that brim. I've seen smaller beach umbrellas. What's up with that?"

"What's up with what?"

"The old Adonis Licht, he'd be thinking, *Can't get too much sun. Melanomas and all that.* Not the new one. The new Adonis belongs to the world. Part of it, anyway. He wants to be seen."

"You're sure about that?"

Fred wagged his finger. "There are things you're not telling me. Especially about you and women. But you *will.* Eventually. If we still have jobs. If *I* still have a job. No one's getting rid of the Museum Man." He slammed an open palm against his forehead. "You called me here to tell me I'm history."

"I didn't call you here. You just showed up."

"The Latinos. They always let us go first."

"You don't think you're getting a little overwrought?"

Fred shrugged. "Anyway, nice hat."

By late-morning, Adonis had accomplished little verging on nothing. Fred's comments had left him unsettled. He couldn't escape worrying that instructions to see Human Resources would show up on Fred's email by lunchtime. But he had greater concerns than Fred. In a few days or even several weeks, the same email could just as easily come his own way once Hunter and Tyler finished buying his silence. A trip to the Museum café seemed a good idea. He rose from his chair.

Lenore Josephson appeared in his doorway. She motioned him to sit back down then closed the door. "We need to talk."

Adonis glanced over Lenore's shoulder for the security guards who would march him out of the building.

She sat and placed a folder on his desk.

"How much time do I have to clear out my things?" he asked.

She raised an eyebrow then burst into laughter. "Oh my God, I wish I had your sense of humor, Adonis. Your timing. That deadpan delivery. You could do stand-up. We'd lose you to TV or Vegas or whatever, but it would almost be worth it."

Adonis stared at the folder.

"It's your statement. Carla Parsont called. The newspaper's going to break the story about Mary-Louise online. This afternoon. They can't hold off."

Adonis ran his fingertip along the folder's edge.

"You're a very valuable resource, Adonis. And you know what makes you so valuable? The humility you express. People in your position, particularly when they rise as fast as you have, they tend to go off the rails."

Adonis wondered if he might be keeping his job. For the moment at any rate.

She tapped the folder. "I've given Carla statements from Hunter and Tyler. We worked them out last night before we brought you into this. Hunter and Tyler will play to the Board, our major donors and our corporate sponsors. The art crowd and the society crowd, too. But we can't discount our members and the public, most of whom don't give a rat's ass about Hunter and Tyler. They don't even know who they are. They need to hear from the Museum Man."

Adonis opened the folder.

"Read it," she said. "Out loud. Connect the words from your brain to your lips."

The Museum is saddened by Dr. Gelderode's resignation. Regrettably, she crossed a line. Dr. Gelderode understands that no institution can permit such behavior from a senior staff member no matter how valuable her professional contributions. Nonetheless, the public can expect the Museum to move forward regardless of this unfortunate betrayal of the Museum's confidence. Brighter days lie ahead.

Lenore tugged at the thin gold chain around her neck. "I hope you're comfortable with that."

"It feels a little stiff. I could..."

Her eyes lit up. "I wouldn't ordinarily say this, but if you feel inspired, go for it. What matters is that the public gets a statement from *you*. That is, the Museum Man."

"The thing is, *betrayal* seems a little harsh."

"Look, no one's happy about all this. But no one ever suggested to Mary-Louise that she get involved with Clark Merrill. What I wrote about going over the line..."

"Crossing the line. A red line, I suppose."

"A red line. Yes. There's an image of wrongdoing there. A violation of trust. People respond to that but only if you back it up, which we have. Anyway, you get my point. Just call Carla when we're finished here. She expects you to."

"I need a few minutes. You can wait here if you like, or I can let you know when I'm ready and you can come back."

She stood. "If you were anyone else, I'd stay. The way it is, you're *not*." She cradled the doorknob in her hand. "Look, the story's set. We can live with it. This is just a simple charm offensive. Charm, Adonis. Don't worry about turning it on. It's always just there."

"It's a shame," Adonis told Carla Parsont ten minutes later.

"So that's it?" she asked. "That's your statement?"

He paused. Then the words rushed out of their own accord. As in the past, they left him unsure they were his. "What I mean is, it's a shame when someone's heart gets the better of them in a difficult situation. You're not always sure what it is you want or how to handle things, but your heart just goes its own way. Aren't we all like that at some time or other?" Adonis waited for Carla's response. "Are you still on the phone?" he asked.

"Yes, of course," she said. "That was so sweet."

Adonis had no idea how Hunter and Tyler would respond to what he'd just said, assuming Carla would quote him accurately. Not that it would matter once everything played out. The situation was being manipulated from the top, and all he could do on his own behalf was buy time. "Anyway," he said, "that *is* my statement. So, can I... can I ask you something?"

"As long as we can end this conversation in sixty seconds. I have to get this story to my editor like now."

"I was thinking... I know you're a journalist, and journalists have standards. You wouldn't want to cross any line like Mary-Louise did. But still, the way the heart wants what it wants and all... I'm wondering if we could go to dinner sometime soon. Just like regular people."

"A date?"

"Yes."

"Could I write about it? My date with the Museum Man? We could also do a video."

"I'm being serious."

"*I'm* being serious. I could bring my fiancé, too. It would be like a reality TV show."

Adonis felt like an orphan abandoned in a forest at midnight. Then a stream of light burst through the entwined branches like a dozen full moons lighting a path before him. Carla was putting him on and in a provocative way. She was telling him in so many words, *I think you're interesting. I know I've held you off with some ridiculous pretext involving professional ethics, but that was just to give myself time to think. What I've concluded is, this could go somewhere. You and me. If you want it to. It's up to you.* Encouraged, he searched for a response. Carla had spoken in a sort of code to force him to express his interest. More than that, to pursue her. Because as best he understood these things, women, even when they protested otherwise, wanted to be pursued. "I guess you've been hiding that ring he gave you."

"Not exactly," she said. "I didn't get it until Friday night just before we got to his parents' house."

24

week later, ignoring the lights and the camera, Adonis studied *The Madonna of the Heavenly Palace* as if seeing it for the first time. An image of Carla Parsont flashed through his mind. Carla holding a baby. *His* baby? But that fantasy had crashed and burned a week before. Or had it been two? Time seemed to be folding in on itself. He focused on the painting, remembering the director's instructions. *Caress the painting with your eyes. Think of Mary as the most desirable woman in the world. A woman of mystery. A frickin' ten. And remember, this painting is more real than real. It's all about beauty and truth, right?*

Adonis took a breath and turned to the camera. "It's a fake but an incredible fake. And it's more. It's a story of humanity's deepest emotions, the highest and the lowest. Come explore it. And enter a whole new reality." He paused, his gaze locked on to the camera lens.

"Cut!" called the director, an auteur in jeans with ripped knees and a black tee shirt emblazoned with the name of an obscure Polish rock band. His alligator cowboy boots nimbly two-stepped around the small set assembled in the Museum's basement. "That's beautiful. Oh, my god. I want to see this show then see it again. And again. Somebody get me tickets."

Jordan Marcus and Nicole Geyer stood with Lenore Josephson by the video monitor. Broad smiles displayed their enthusiasm.

"Uh, Tony," Adonis asked the director. "Do you think maybe that was a little..."

"I loved it," said Tony. "Let's take a look."

"I'll put sound on the speaker," said the audio engineer. Adonis remembered his name as Curt. Adonis Licht had difficulty with people's names, but the Museum Man could no more forget them than a politician at a fundraiser could suffer a memory lapse—or lack an aide at his ear.

"Roger that, good buddy," said Tony. He displayed a grin the Cheshire Cat might have envied. On the set, everyone was a best friend, every act a cause for congratulations and celebration.

Adonis studied himself on the screen studying the painting. They'd shot only three takes. He'd anticipated shooting would consume the entire morning. For starters, this was all new to him. He'd never been in TV commercials for his parents' stores. Added to that, he'd slept no more than two or three hours the night before, although he'd awakened alert and ready to go as always. Then, on the set, Jordan and Tony dwelled on every detail. *You have to respect your oeuvre. It's your legacy.* More, the scene was being shot out of sequence. Shooting schedules, it seemed, paid no heed to chronology. *Nothing about shooting a commercial or a film for that matter has anything to do with reality,* Tony explained. *We're in the business of illusion. Illusion and emotion.*

Other scenes, all without dialogue, would establish a mood of mystery and anticipation before the payoff they'd just shot. The camera would track the Museum Man making his way through dimly lit hallways, descending staircases and opening a series of doors like a movie hero in search of priceless treasures navigating the labyrinth of an ancient king's newly unearthed tomb. After lunch, the camera crew would shoot various close-ups of Adonis on his subterranean adventures. The remainder of the afternoon would involve a double appearing in dimly lit long and medium shots revealing only the Museum Man's back or silhouette.

Tony turned to Jordan and Nicole. "Tell me you wouldn't buy a used car from this guy."

"What can I say?" said Jordan. "The Museum Man could sell sand in the Sahara."

A member of the crew handed the painting to a Museum staff member. The piece itself was an illusion—a digital copy of the fake Norbertus in a frame crafted in the Museum's atelier to resemble the original—itself a fake dating from the mid-eighteenth century. Hunter Kirk had insisted that *The Madonna of the Heavenly Palace* not be exposed to the production company's lighting or compromised in any other way. *Too valuable. Not as valuable as if it was real, but a fake this good... if Clark Merrill wants it back... could go at auction for over a million dollars. Otherwise, we'll deaccession it. The lawyers can work it out.*

Adonis knew that masterly fakes could have significant value based on the stories behind them. *The Madonna of the Heavenly Palace* offered a tale of superb craftsmanship by an unknown artist. Mary-Louise's seemingly sordid indiscretion with Clark Merrill—or Clark Merrill's sordid indiscretion with Mary-Louise—enhanced the story. Moreover, the *mea culpa* pronounced by the Museum Man along with his announcement of an exhibition on fakes had burnished the reputation of the Museum, now positioned as victim rather than villain.

The Museum Man also had made another announcement should anyone doubt the Museum's integrity. A generous donor pledged to fund an investigation to uncover the artist who had usurped Norbertus of Hannover. A noted filmmaker would document the inquiry with the goal of obtaining widespread theatrical and cable release. The Museum would host the film's premier.

Advance ticket sales soared.

Then there was the call from Apollo. *You are some frickin' piece of work. Does this make sense to you? This makes no sense to me. I hope they're paying you extra for all this PR shit. You getting any TV offers? If you're not, get your head out of your ass. Hire an agent. They should be swarming all over you. You should have an agent. I bet you don't. Schmuck, everyone loves the Museum Man. But don't bullshit me. I'm your brother. You're still Adonis Licht. But I'm thinking, you could be in my company's TV commercials. We'd give you stock. Theoretically, I mean. I can't say we're going public soon. The SEC would be all over my ass. For the record, I'm not saying it. But if we* did, *your stock could be worth big bucks. What's the Museum paying you? What's that word Grandpa used to use?* Bupkes. *It means* nothing. *I think it means shit or goat shit or something like that. So you're getting what now? Bupkes, right? You never gave a shit about money. How about women, though? What kind of stuff are you bagging? I've got my hands full at home. You have one kid, the sex goes downhill. Two kids? Over a cliff. You get a little on the side, you keep it quiet. Nobody's hurt. But you? You're a free man. You can have all the pussy you want. Or maybe I've got you wrong. Do I have you wrong? Anyway, Mom's thinking about having all of us over to the estate for Thanksgiving. That's what? Four months off? Five? Make some money by then or don't bother coming. We're winners. Lichts are winners. Then there's you. Or there* was *you.*

Adonis stood with Lenore and Jordan and Nicole and Tony and—what was his name? Curt. They watched the take he'd just recorded.

Tony and Jordan each clapped him on the back.

"Okay, let's take a break for an early lunch," said Tony. "We have tables reserved in the members dining room. We're eating with the Museum Man, right?"

Lenore grasped Jordan's elbow. "Just a reminder. In post-production, make sure you get Adonis' new title right."

25

F red ran interference for Adonis as they snaked their way to the restaurant's paneled bar area where brass fittings and cut-glass fixtures flaunted retro elegance. Catching the eye of a bartender who might have been an aspiring actress, he called out, "Manhattans. Two."

Adonis' eyes swept the crowd. He'd spent little time with people like them. In truth, no time. Except at the gym. They probably all worked out. The women wore figure revealing skirts or slacks with blouses open two or more buttons. The men, in jeans and fitted shirts, looked somewhat more casual but no less intent on making an impression. He watched heads swivel to survey prospects or competition then bob to indicate agreement or laughter or both. Registering an eight seemed the minimum requirement for entry.

"One of the hottest places in the city," said Fred.

Adonis offered a half-hearted nod. He had no idea why he'd let Fred talk him into coming here.

The bartender set down two Manhattans. The liquid appeared a shade paler than the red cherry at the bottom of each glass. A strip of orange peel caressed each rim.

Fred handed Adonis his cocktail.

Adonis followed Fred's lead and sipped. His eyebrows arched.

Fred grinned. "The best Manhattans in the city, that's for sure." He lowered his glass. "It's all about premium bourbon."

"I don't know," said Adonis.

"You don't know what? If this is a kick-ass cocktail?"

"I've never had a Manhattan. And aren't cocktails supposed to be fattening?"

"Jesus, you're a fucking virgin."

"I think maybe I should get a glass of wine."

Fred shook his head. "A guy like you?"

Adonis placed his free hand over his ear and rubbed. He wasn't used to music and conversation ricocheting off walls and ceilings at hormone rousing levels.

Fred raised his glass to his lips. "We're celebrating you being a TV star for shit's sake!" he shouted. "And your promotion!"

"So how come *I* have to pay for dinner?"

"You're making more money than God is why?"

"Not as much as Mary-Louise made. I'm sure of that."

Fred sipped and lowered his glass. "All I know is, I did *my* job. I'm the one who suggested we go out instead of you holing up in your studio."

An attractive woman approached. The shiny fabric of her periwinkle blouse accentuated her breasts and complemented her long blonde hair. She smiled then continued in the direction of the restrooms.

"I think I'm in love," said Fred.

"She's probably here with a date."

"Or friends. Real women looking for real men."

"So where does that leave *you*?" Adonis asked.

Fred put up a hand as if he'd been sucker-punched and sought to avoid another blow.

"I didn't mean that the way it sounded," said Adonis. He rested his elbow on the bar. The lone sip he'd taken of the Manhattan wasn't making him woozy, but he didn't feel exactly comfortable. Maybe it was the crowd, jammed shoulder to shoulder. And the elevated decibel level. Of course, that was no excuse for insulting Fred. Although who had the woman smiled at anyway? He and Fred averaged an eight—if Fred was a six. But Fred might be right. Why couldn't they strike up a conversation and invite two beautiful women to dinner? He'd treat. He might not be earning Mary-Louise's salary given the years she'd held the Curator in Charge position, but he was making a lot more money than he'd ever dreamed of.

"No hard feelings," Fred said. "The way I see it, the Museum Man is gonna attract some fine-looking women. Whatever you leave over is still going to be prime."

"Millet's *The Gleaners*," Adonis said.

"Jesus, turn it off. We're here to drink and eat and drink and maybe get laid. Anyway, Millet's nineteenth-century. We do the Renaissance thing."

Surveying the bodies packed in front of him, Adonis wondered whether he should be selecting a woman from among several small groups expecting, he assumed, to meet men. Apollo would have targeted a woman on entering the room. The role of predator made Adonis uncomfortable, even if hooking up was a game everyone played. He imagined he'd feel more relaxed after an introduction, but getting to that point remained a fearsome challenge. He'd developed a reasonable comfort level with women approaching him, but those encounters took place in more sober environments. He turned his attention to the restaurant area, hoping their table would be ready soon. Then, not knowing what else to say to Fred, he turned to take in the other end of the bar.

The blonde woman who'd smiled in his direction—at *him*—walked towards them.

"Hi," Fred said.

She turned to Adonis. "Aren't you...?"

Adonis took a breath.

"No," she said. "You can't be."

"Can't be what?" said Fred. "Or who?"

Adonis' fingertips pressed into his palms.

Her eyes sparkled despite the sole illumination at the bar being that which lit the bottles behind it. "On second thought you look awfully like..."

Fred raised his glass. "The new Curator in Charge of Renaissance Art at one of the world's foremost museums not to mention one of the city's newest and biggest celebrities."

"I hope I didn't insult you," she said. "My not being sure you were... But... Oh my god... You *are*. The Museum Man!" She raised her hand to her fuchsia-pink lips, revealing matching fingernails, then let it drop. "I feel like an idiot. Shouldn't I know your name?"

"Adonis."

"Adonis? Really?"

A square-jawed man joined them. "Table's ready."

"Go ahead," said the woman. "I'll be there in a minute. This is the Museum Man."

"The who?" the man asked.

"Those ads when you go online? And the buses? His picture's all over the buses. And posters? They're everywhere."

The young man clutched the woman by the arm. "Rich and Suzanne are waiting."

She shook her arm free. "Can I ask you a question?" she said to Adonis.

The young man pulled her towards him.

"Jesus, Scott!" she protested.

Throughout the bar, voices hushed.

"Hey," said Fred, "she just wants to ask the Museum Man a question."

"Fuck you!" the man shouted.

"Fuck *you!*" Fred returned.

Adonis held his right palm out. "I'm sorry. He didn't mean anything."

The man shoved Fred against the bar. Fred's cocktail spilled across his lap and splashed the woman's blouse.

"What is wrong with you Scott?" the woman cried out.

The man pushed her aside and confronted Adonis. "Museum fucker? Is that you? Trying to pick up other guys' dates or what?"

Adonis sensed everything around him slowing while at the same time, each face and feature in the bar came into greater focus. "I think your table is ready," he said with a calm deliberation that surprised him. "I think your date would like to have dinner now."

The man's right fist drifted towards him.

Adonis raised his left arm to block the punch then threw his right.

Bone crunched. The man tumbled backward. He landed on a small table where a couple barely managed to evade his collapsed body. Blood trickled down his chin. His eyes resembled those of a fish on a bed of ice.

Adonis examined his fist. He'd never thrown a punch before.

"Maybe," said Fred, "we should eat someplace else."

Hunter Kirk held up his cell phone. "This thing at that bar last night? It's gone viral, you know."

"I wasn't thinking," said Adonis.

Hunter Kirk leaned across his desk. "Of course, you weren't thinking. A punch like that, you don't think. You react." He placed the phone down. "You have a brother?"

"An older brother."

"He ever beat on you?"

"A little."

"I have an older sister. Five years. She whipped my ass until I was about ten."

"Did you get too big?"

"I grew late. She stopped wailing on me because she wanted to protect her hands."

Adonis stood in silence.

"You ever need your brain taken apart, Dr. Gwendolyn Kirk Thomas is your neurosurgeon."

Adonis wondered where the conversation was going, although having been summoned to Dr. Kirk's office, he'd anticipated what he thought would be its purpose. "I owe the Museum an apology. And you, of course."

"Is that it? You punch someone out in a bar, and you want to apologize?"

"I've drafted my resignation. I didn't know if you'd want an email or a printed copy, but you can have either as soon as I get to my office. My *old* office."

Hunter Kirk walked around the desk and tapped Adonis lightly on the jaw. "If it comes to it, we'll bring in the Museum's law firm, and no one in their right mind would fuck with them. But I doubt we'll have a problem. Whoever took that video posted the whole story. That guy shoved del Campo. He shoved the woman. And he threw the first punch." He held up Adonis' right hand. "Damn. Not even a bruise. Anyway, I've been getting emails. The Museum Man's a hero." He wrapped an arm around Adonis' shoulders and squeezed. "You can't buy publicity like that."

26

Staying home that night seemed the prudent thing to do, yet Adonis found himself as uncomfortable as if he'd opened himself up to continued public scrutiny. Turning off the lamp next to the sofa, he let a used paperback of Kafka's *The Metamorphosis* slip to the floor. A gnawing feeling of apprehension made more unnerving by the unseasonable heat rendered it impossible to concentrate on the plight of Gregor Samsa.

He flipped open his laptop, hoping that emails and social media might keep his mind occupied. He contemplated scanning the news, but he could only digest so much of that. Hours earlier, he'd abandoned any possibility of trying to keep up with his professional reading.

The corner of the screen displayed 1:23 AM. Despite his discomfort, his lips turned up in a wry smile. One-two-three. What a simple, elemental number. And how cruel. Late hours had become his new normal, something of a return to his college routine. Although at school he'd been the kind of student who drifted off not long past midnight while others engaged in bullshit sessions or crammed for exams. Now, he couldn't enjoy more than three hours sleep. Still, that was all he needed.

Just past two, Adonis slipped into bed. The waning moon had all but vanished. Several minutes later, he sat up, stripped off his sweat-soaked tee shirt and kicked the sheet that had covered him towards the foot of the bed. He lay back down. Sleep seemed distant, bent on eluding him. He attempted a visualization. He grasped a large knife then raised it towards a bunch of balloons that represented his swarming thoughts. Slowly, he severed each string tethering a thought to his restless mind. Despite his continued efforts, each time a balloon sailed off, another took its place. He wielded the knife at an ever-faster pace, demonstrating an unsettling ferocity. After freeing the last balloon, he drifted off.

At three-thirty, a storm pried open Adonis' eyes. Raindrops clattered against the windowpanes like buckshot. He leaped from bed and closed the window. Gale winds rattled the panes like a sugar-saturated toddler shaking a colorfully wrapped package. Lightning set the night aglow as if the city had fallen under aerial bombardment. Thunderclaps suggested entire neighborhoods being reduced to rubble. Although the window remained closed, the apartment rapidly cooled. He returned to bed and pulled the sheet over his shoulders. The lullaby of the storm returned him to sleep.

The storm passed. The quiet wrenched Adonis awake again. His cell displayed 4:25. He turned on the radio. A news feature reported the astonishing rise of the Museum Man. He changed the station, hoping that music would provide a soothing distraction. He remained awake, twisted in the sheet and near writhing like Rubens' Baroque Prometheus, chained to a rock, an eagle feeding on his liver each day as punishment for bringing fire to mankind. Disconnected thoughts multiplied like bacteria in a Petri dish.

As the sun hovered above the lower rooflines across the street, Adonis went to the bathroom. He considered his reflection in the mirror like a visitor to the Museum contemplating a portrait by Bellini or Holbein. He pressed his fingertips against the mirror's smooth surface.

A new reality confronted him. The Museum Man was nothing more than a museum piece to be admired from a distance. He could easily have been chiseled from marble, a variation of Duquesnoy's *Adonis* restored from a Roman torso and completed to assume the identity of the god—a work warming the imagination but cold to the touch.

The next morning, half-heartedly spooning sections of grapefruit, Adonis decided to pass on his morning workout. Instead, he'd take a circuitous route to the Museum to observe the wakening city. Halfway down the stairs, he changed his mind. If he failed to maintain his schedule at the gym, he'd arouse suspicions and likely become the target of rumors. No one would believe he could maintain a body so lean, muscular and fit without intense daily workouts. Or drugs. Speculation would fester. Lies would erupt like boils and spread through cyberspace like a contagion with no cure. He feared that the one thing people liked more than creating celebrities was destroying them.

At a quarter to six, Adonis walked into a packed locker room. Someone had notified the world where the Museum Man worked out. Greetings flew at him from all directions. Rob had to escort him to the weight room through a phalanx of well-wishers. Applause accompanied his cardio.

Showered and dressed, Adonis entered the lobby. Well-wishers offered their hands. At the door, he put on his sunglasses and hat. Outside, the air remained cool and invigorating. People acknowledged each other with a wave or a nod. Morning traffic spurned its usual impatience. Taxi drivers resisted pounding their horns. The city could well have been coming to life on a computer screen with the volume lowered.

Adonis ducked into the covered entryway of a still-closed men's shirt store and reached into his jacket pocket. From a small plastic packet, he withdrew a false mustache purchased online. He could have gone to a downtown costume shop, but that kind of visibility risked exposure. The Museum Man disguising himself? Halloween was months off. Was some further scandal brewing? Unless the Museum Man had been invited to a costume gala. Or had a bloated ego turned him into one of those celebrities who crave recognition but reject those who offer it? Ego, he noted to himself, had nothing to do with it.

Adonis pressed the mustache against his upper lip and started counting. At twenty, he lowered his hand. He twitched his nose. Tensed his cheeks. The mustache held. He studied his dim reflection in the glass of the front door. Did he look like someone wearing one of those fake disguises complete with oversized nose? Not quite. His nose belonged more to Michelangelo's David than to some old-time comedian. To all appearances, he was a man with a luxuriant mustache stretching from one corner of his mouth to the other. He nodded to his image.

A breeze blew gently at Adonis' back while the sun cast the kind of golden glow achieved only in films by a cinematographer's carefully chosen lens or digital enhancement. The air appeared so crystalline that Adonis feared the least disturbance would cause it to shatter. He looked up. The sky, as well as the buildings above him, seemed free of pigeons. He looked down. The sidewalks appeared unnaturally clean as if an unseen army of Russian babushkas had wielded brooms and hoses through the night, leaving every corner of the city as spotless as a theme park.

For that matter, a fairy godmother might have sprinkled the city with the stuff of primal happiness.

His spirits rising, Adonis detoured to a café he visited only on occasion. He ordered two lattes. Thinking that Anna might appreciate a small deviation from the routine, he asked for two banana-walnut muffins. The barista's smile betrayed no hint of recognition. Delighted, Adonis dropped a five-dollar bill into the tip jar. The barista thanked him profusely.

An odd thought struck Adonis as he left. Perhaps the same unknown force that transformed the city overnight might produce a change in his appearance as dramatic as that in his mood. Out of kindness—or pity—it might restore him to some semblance of his former self the way a stretched rubber band, once released, contracts to its original length and shape. He acknowledged that being a ten had its rewards, but he would welcome being a four or even a three—a prince turned back into a frog both wiser and happier.

He strolled towards Anna's alley.

A massive flock of pigeons appeared overhead. It came close to blotting out the sun.

Traffic slowed, thickened and clotted into a bottleneck. Pedestrians resumed their normal hurried pace, brushed shoulders, bellowed impatience.

The pigeons streamed off.

Adonis spotted familiar flashing red and blue lights. He approached three—no, four—police cruisers straddling the street and sidewalk in front of the alley. They formed a perimeter around a fire-rescue truck and an ambulance. Uniformed officers stood in front of a strand of yellow tape, holding at bay a small knot of onlookers.

He worked his way forward. Inside the alley, several men and a woman with short brown hair—all wearing civilian clothes and white medical gloves—hovered over what appeared to be a body covered by a yellow tarp. Adonis assumed them to be detectives. Behind them, two paramedics packed their gear while a young man in a short-sleeved shirt and khakis took photographs. An older man in a gray suit tucked a laptop into a battered carrying case. Adonis conjectured he was a medical examiner.

The woman detective waved. The uniformed officers pulled up on the yellow tape. Ambulance personnel hunched over and entered with a wheeled cart.

The officers gestured for the small crowd to step back.

The ambulance attendants rolled the cart out of the alley. As they lifted the cart to slide it through the vehicle's open rear doors, a bit of the yellow tarp fell away.

Adonis saw a black-gloved hand.

27

"Slept in?" Fred asked as Adonis entered his office. "It's getting to be lunchtime."

Adonis considered how to explain Anna. How to explain wandering the streets all morning. He saw no option but to offer Fred an explanation he could understand. "I worked at home last night. I thought I could use a little extra sleep."

"You sleep through that storm? I was drawing plans for an ark. I pretty much stayed awake until my alarm went off then hit it running. Some of us can go short on sleep and still punch in on time."

Adonis sat at his desk. "We're museum curators, Fred. We don't punch time clocks."

"My dad punched in at the machine shop. My grandfather's shop. While he was going to school. Degree in accounting. He became a CPA. Opened a small firm or practice or whatever you call it. If the Museum Man needs his taxes done..."

"Isn't this about the time you head down to the café?"

"You're not trying to get rid of me, are you?" Fred's jaw dropped. "Shit! You partied last night is what you did. That video from the bar. You've got women camping out in front of your building. I bet she was hot. Forget about a ten. An eleven!"

Adonis brought up his email.

"Look, I get it. Even the Museum Man runs out of gas after spending the night with a super-hot woman. Or two. Damn, you had two babes at your place, right? I bet you skipped the gym this morning, huh?"

Adonis closed his eyes. "You're sure you're not headed to the café?"

Fred's grin wilted. "Sometimes I think you turn me off. Like I'm a light bulb. You want the room dark, you flip the switch. What I'm saying is, you don't listen to me."

Adonis opened his eyes. "I listen to you Fred."

"And I'm supposed to believe that why? Because you're my boss? Not that far back, we shared office space. Our desks were pushed together. And you know what? Even then, you never listened. Not really."

"I listened."

"Everyone needs to be listened to," said Fred. "I mean, what's art?" He rubbed his back against the doorpost. "I'm serious. Art's all about connections, right? Art creates this connection between you and something outside yourself. Or deep inside. That probably sounds like I'm talking about the Church, but I'm not. Although it's close to the same thing. Art and religion. Religion creating art. I wrote an undergrad paper on that. All I'm saying is, everyone needs someone to listen."

Adonis watched Fred's face dissolve into Anna's, his eyes now hers inviting him to confide what he could tell no one else. He bit his lips.

"I don't know where you are," said Fred, "but it isn't here." He made two fists and tapped them together. "So okay, *now* I'm going to the café."

Adonis listened to Fred's retreating footsteps then closed the door. His shoulders slumped. He was, at least nominally, Fred's manager, and he'd blown it. He hadn't given Fred whatever it was he needed. What that might be, he had no idea. Probably Fred had no idea. Which brought up an intriguing question. What did Adonis Licht need?

In the hours since seeing Anna's body removed from the alley, he'd felt like a ship sailing a rocky coastline through a thick fog, his compass on the blink, his sense of direction lost. Only when he entered the Museum did it occur to him that he hadn't asked the police what had happened. Anna certainly could have died from natural causes. Living on the street had to shorten anyone's life. But Anna's suffering a fatal heart attack or a stroke failed to explain the crime-scene photographer. Unless that was standard procedure. In death, as in life, Anna remained a mystery.

Adonis went to the website of the city's dominant news-radio station and clicked on the live audio broadcast. Stories about bodies found in alleys merited airtime. People consumed reports about murders, car crashes and other gory tragedies the way they devoured popcorn in movie theaters. He reflected that they might even have good reason. The news provided a measure of relief. They'd survived the perils of the world—at least so far that day. Another thought struck Adonis. It walked a line between frivolous and profound. The same horrible news offered a bright side. The media provided victims lacking family and friends with a measure of acknowledgement, no matter how brief, before the world erased them from its collective memory.

Leaving the broadcast on, Adonis returned to his email. Human Resources had copied him on résumés forwarded to Tyler Severinsen. Given the speed with which Adonis had been promoted, Tyler was taking it upon himself to choose the department's new Assistant Curator. The position required significant management skills. *You're not just the head of the Department of Renaissance Art,* Tyler had explained, *you're the face of the Museum. We can't burden you with administrative work.*

DAVID PERLSTEIN

The news anchor drew his attention. *Murder in a downtown alley. But first...*

Anna *had* been murdered—assuming only one murder in a downtown alley had taken place in the last twelve hours or so. Details, of course, would be delayed. The station's revenue depended on advertisers selling free-range chicken parts, replacement windows, relief for upset stomachs and pickup trucks. Adonis kept an ear cocked. A casino promised to give away substantial sums of cash each hour and a new car on Saturdays at midnight. A cell phone carrier pledged the best coverage in the area. A deep-voiced announcer, in the threatening tone of a mob boss, hawked a cockroach spray. *Makes 'em dead. Keeps 'em dead.*

When the news resumed, Adonis trembled.

During the night, an unidentified homeless woman appearing to be about seventy years old suffered multiple fatal stab wounds. A sanitation worker called police.

The Mayor responded. *This terrible crime represents an anomaly. During my administration, we've cut the city's homicide rate by eight-point-six percent. We've decreased our homeless rate by five-point-nine percent. We are committed to keeping this city safe. Rest assured, we will bring the murderer to justice.*

Overcome by exhaustion—to which he had thought himself immune—Adonis clicked off the station, let his eyelids drop and drifted off. A chill woke him. His eyes shot open. For a fragment of a second—perhaps no more than a sixtieth—he found himself submersed in a blackness unlike anything he'd ever experienced. A complete absence of light. Utter nothingness. A void. Then he vaulted back into the world like a circus performer shot out of a cannon.

He checked his laptop. He'd napped for almost an hour.

Still, he couldn't help thinking that he hadn't so much slept as experienced a taste of death.

28

The waiter, a regular in the members dining room, smiled at Adonis then placed the dinner check in front of Carla Parsont. She picked it up and looked at Adonis. "You've seemed a little... I'd say *down,* but I can't imagine the Museum Man being down. Distracted? Is that fair?"

"Fair enough," said Adonis. Naturally, he hadn't mentioned Anna during the interview. He had no intention of bringing her up now. Fred's words came to him. *Everyone needs somebody to listen.* Anna had been that person for him. But the Museum Man and a bag lady? A *murdered* bag lady? He couldn't possibly reveal to Carla something that would position him on the spectrum of irrationality. Probably at one of its extremities.

"You're not bothered that *I'm* paying for our meals, are you?" she asked.

"You explained journalistic integrity before as I remember."

"Not that it costs me anything. Expense account. Or what passes for one. They watch every penny. A Sunday magazine profile? All business."

Adonis sipped the last of his coffee. "I get it. Really."

She smiled. "If anyone understands, it's the Museum Man. But I hope I wasn't a pain in the ass asking you too many questions. You know, about what it's like being you and what you do. Being the face of the Museum and all that."

"I enjoyed it. Really. And it's a good thing we got together so early." He looked past her. The dining room glowed.

"The way it stays light so late this time of year," Carla said. "I'm not sure if I like that. I'm a night person."

"I know how that goes. Anyway, I appreciate it being an early evening and all. The closer we get to the Madonna and Child exhibition, the more work we all have."

She lifted her napkin and dabbed at the corners of her mouth. "By the way, your mother is very proud."

Adonis tensed. Having lulled him all through dinner and coaxed him to bury any last vestige of romantic feelings, she was circling in for the kill. He assumed she'd seen "before" photos and gathered salient details about his childhood. Now, she would probe his transformation into the Museum Man. And where would that lead? How would she—would anyone—ever make sense of a mystery as impenetrable as it had become vexing. Of necessity, he'd be vague. Still, she might expose him as a man best suited to a carnival side show. "You spoke with my mother?"

"She thinks you're wonderful, but I'm sure you know that."

Adonis willed his composure to return. "All mothers feel that way." He seized the opportunity to launch a probe of his own. "She must have told you a lot. Stories, I mean. About when I was a kid."

"Your childhood? I know where you went to school. You liked to draw and paint. You weren't into sports, although fitness is something else. Sometimes, people get the bug late, you know? But that stuff just sets the stage. Our readers don't care about Adonis Licht. All they want to know is what it's like being the Museum Man."

As the car Carla summoned disappeared in traffic, Adonis turned back to the plaza in front of the Museum. Having told the truth about being busier than ever, it only made sense to get some work done before going home.

A woman across the plaza drew his attention. Seated on a bench, she appeared slim and graceful in the demi-light. Adonis noted the hem of her ivory-colored dress settled just above her knees. Despite the early-evening warmth, a white scarf draped her shoulders. An elegant hat covered her head. In contrast with the light, summer colors of her dress and scarf, the hat appeared to be scarlet. Considerably larger than his own, it no doubt served the same purpose, defending her not only against the intrusion of the sun now hidden behind neighboring buildings but also the unwanted glances of others.

Adonis remained at the curb transfixed. He wondered whether Anna once resembled that woman. Whether she also had experienced a transformation, only in reverse.

The last remnant of the day created a sky blending amethyst with violet-blue. Lights blinked on. Sculpture-quality fixtures bathed the plaza in an artificial radiance extending a welcome to evening visitors and a promise of safe passage to those strolling by.

The woman in the crimson hat rose, held a straw handbag by her side and faced the Museum entry as if standing before the altar in a cathedral.

Adonis remained motionless.

After a moment of what could have been taken as devout contemplation, the woman turned and walked away. She displayed a familiar limp.

Having passed on working into the evening, Adonis unlocked the door to his apartment building. His left hand clutched a small paper bag.

Margaret the Building Manager shut the door to her mailbox. "Worked late again? People must want you for this or that all the time. Me, I just got back from dinner with a friend. We try not to stay out late they way you young people do. Of course, she asked all about you." She spotted the small paper bag. "Been shopping?"

"I had to pick something up on the way home."

She lifted her eyes. "Well, I'm glad I ran into you. I was going to slip a note under your door. It's the apartment. That large corner one-bedroom I've been telling you about. It's coming available the end of next month."

Adonis nodded.

"Of course, we'll spiff up the kitchen for you. New appliances. Granite countertops. Re-do the bathroom. The floors, too. New window coverings. Amazing what new window coverings can do. And paint. We always paint. You can move into a beautiful apartment like you see in those magazines. The kind of apartment everyone expects the Museum Man to live in."

"Thank you," said Adonis, "but I'm still thinking about it."

She stroked her chin. "You're not moving out, are you?"

"No, I'm not leaving. I just... I'm not sure."

"You're not seriously thinking about staying in that studio? It was fine for the old you. Licht three-oh-two. But honestly, *that* guy? Don't get me wrong, but he didn't have much going for him. Not someone you'd give a second thought to, if you know what I mean."

29

Towards midnight, Adonis pushed up the window as far as it would go. An indifferent breeze crawled over the sill. It hinted at another stifling night. He studied the moon, its crescent waning. He felt as lifeless and incomplete as Michelangelo's unfinished *Atlas Slave* with its bare outlines of the Titan held captive in stone and bent beneath the weight of the world.

From the paper bag he'd brought upstairs he withdrew a small, clear glass filled with candle wax and a wick. He set it on his nightstand. Despite its modesty, the *yahrzeit* would pay tribute not only to Anna's death but also to her life. He owed her that. Surely she'd endured great pain. Without question, she'd helped ease *his* pain even if she couldn't rid him of it.

He went to the fridge, took out a bottle of water and ran it across his forehead. Then he returned to the bed and sat by the window. He could have been an old man settled on a park bench with no one to go home to, nothing to differentiate one day from the next. For that matter, he could have been Anna.

After a moment, Adonis kneeled in front of the window and placed the *yahrzeit* on the concrete ledge outside. The candle would be visible only to people in the apartments across the street and at that, they'd have to part their draperies or open their blinds and peer out. But the limited number of human witnesses did not limit the intent of this modest act. The *yahrzeit* would declare its presence to the moon and the stars. Notice would be served to the universe. Attention would be paid.

He struck a match. A flame flared. He reached his hand towards the ledge.

The flapping of wings stopped him. A seemingly familiar pigeon—its head and neck coal black, its body pure white—perched next to the *yahrzeit*.

Adonis blew out the match and snapped off its head. He tossed the wooden remainder onto his nightstand.

The pigeon swung its beak to flick the spent match head off the ledge.

Adonis raised his hand.

The pigeon cocked its head. It seemed to dare him.

He made a fist.

The pigeon held its ground.

He pondered going to the closet for his baseball bat. He concluded that he'd just make a mess. He sighed.

The pigeon cooed softly.

Adonis contemplated the pigeon.

The pigeon contemplated the unlit *yahrzeit*.

"Beat it," he said in a near-whisper demonstrating a clear lack of conviction.

The pigeon cooed again.

Adonis resigned himself to the bird's presence. More, he found himself pleased to have its company. Perhaps, in some peculiar way, they were kindred souls. He lit another match.

The pigeon's gaze followed the flame on its brief but graceful arc towards the *yahrzeit*.

Adonis' hand hesitated near the glass's rim.

The light of the flame revealed the pigeon's eye to be a brilliant blue.

His breathing measured, he nestled the flame against the wick.

The wick resisted.

Adonis held the match in place.

The flame flickered against the wick then blossomed like a wildflower after a springtime shower.

The pigeon stepped towards Adonis.

He blew out the match.

A puff of smoke ascended with the fragility of a soul.

The flame atop the candle swayed like a grief-stricken survivor watching a loved one being lowered into the grave.

Adonis took a deep breath. He held it until release was no longer an option. As he exhaled, he conceded that the light he'd kindled wasn't only for Anna.

ᴀCKNOⲰLEDGⲘENTS

A novel may have a single author, but many people play an important role in its development.

My wife Carolyn, along with Stefan Barkow, Ron Eaton and Jim Shay, read early drafts and provided welcome feedback. Jim also offered valuable expertise on Renaissance architecture.

Reneé Dreyfus, Curator of Ancient Art and Interpretation, the Fine Arts Museums of San Francisco, provided insights on the world of museums.

My son Aaron Perlstein guided me with expert advice on physical and weight training.

As always, Tom Parker, a master teacher of fiction, assisted and inspired me to present the best story in the best form within my abilities.

Aditionally, Noah Charney's fascinating book *The Art of Forgery* proved a marvelous resource for learning about faked art.

Printed in the United States
By Bookmasters